Some of w[...]
saying on meg[...]

" The story is really great and I lo[...]
  - Corey Eindahl

" I loved reading the book you wrote, it was really good. mum kept getting cross at me for not putting it down!"
  - Kate Ilona

" My son went to bed with this book at 7.30pm. I went in to tell him 'lights off' at 8pm, and he asked if he could have another 15 minutes as he just loved the book. I said yes, then went back to our guests that we had over for dinner.
At 8.15pm I then told him to put it away and go to sleep. At 10pm I went back in, and he had got up and started reading again!!! I gave in to him and said that's fine but not much longer!!! At 11.45PM... he was still going!!
Thank you."
  - Tracey Freckelton

" All I would like to say your book is awesome!"
  - Jack Stewart

" I LOVE YOUR NEW BOOK MEGS AND THE VOOTBALL KIDS"
  - Peter Eid

" I was only given Megs 4 days ago and could not stop reading it, and have finished it this morning! Is there going to be another one?"
  - Nathan Bruen

" I have just finished reading your book "Megs and The Vootball Kids" and I enjoyed it very much. It was hard to put down! When is the next book coming out?"
  - Jarrod Hancock

www.megsmorrison.com

For all those Aussie kids, big and small, who have slogged it out on the parched football pitches of Australian suburbia and who, just like me, have dreamed of one day wearing the Green and Gold.

Mark

To the anonymous inventor of the 'nutmeg' – football's icing on top of an already delicious cake.

Neil

& The Vootball Kids

Neil Montagnana Wallace with Mark Schwarzer

www.bouncebooks.com

Copyright © Neil Montagnana Wallace 2007
First published in Australia in 2007 by Bounce Books Pty Ltd.
Reprinted in 2007

National Library of Australia
Cataloguing-in-Publication data:

Montagnana Wallace, Neil.
  Megs & The Vootball Kids

  2nd ed.
  For juveniles.
  ISBN 9780980316704 (pbk.)

  1. Soccer - Australia - Juvenile fiction.
  2. Immigrant children - Australia - Juvenile fiction.
  I. Schwarzer, Mark. II. Title.
A823.4

Cover illustration by Daniel Tonkin, Iron Monkey Studios
(www.ironmonkeystudios.com)

Cover design by Leonard Montagnana, Woof Creative Solutions
(www.woof.com.au)

Internal design by Woof Creative Solutions

Back Cover photography by Tim Clayton & Lindsay McNeill.

Internal Schwarzer photography by Tim Clayton and from the family collection.

Edited by Gwenda Smyth

Distributed in Australia by Macmillan Distribution (www.macmillan.com.au)

Printed and bound by Tien Wah Press (PTE) Limited

www.bouncebooks.com

Mark's Shout-outs

There was many a time when I could have quite easily been lured to play the more popular codes of the day such as cricket or rugby league. So a huge thanks to my parents for helping me to keep sight of my football dreams. I'm grateful for their single-mindedness in supporting the hobby that has become my passion as well as my career.

Neil's Shout-outs

Val comes first because she always will. A critical eye, some expert advice and an outstanding ability to cook pancakes are just the beginning. Walking home from school reading a book doesn't seem so strange to me now, kid.

Thanks to the Schwarzers for being so open and enthusiastic. Professional football is a team game off the pitch as much as on, and Team Schwarzer gets my ongoing admiration.

To Leonard for his enthusiasm, skill and talent. The clients come for the design, but they stay for the package. Bounce Books and Woof Creative are in safe hands.

Cheers to Dan from Iron Monkey Studios. You've brought Megs to a new range of senses.

Mark Haldane and Macmillan Distribution have been outstanding right from the start. And Gwenda – you are an editor extraordinaire.

Val's Grade 5VM-W at Essendon North Primary all get my thanks too – for being the guinea pigs, and for doing their bit to help. Likewise to all the family and friends who took the time and gave me feedback along the way. Especially the real Jo Sheather.

And finally, a massive thank you to The Bean for pushing me on and firing me up. Yours will be a life worth living, baby Finn.

Foreword

For me, football started out as something to pass the time. I grew up in the western suburbs of Sydney, far away from the distractions of the city. Out west, most kids played sport in their free time. There were few cinemas, skating rinks, bowling complexes or Time Zones – the diversions available to city kids. And in the 'old' days there were no Play Stations, X boxes, PSPs, email, mobile phones or computers. Moreover, money was tight. I was the second child of German immigrants who had come to Australia in the mid-60s in search of adventure and a better life.

Enter football, the one thing I could do that my parents supported, that was free, and that truly gave me a buzz. I still grin from ear to ear as I remember those uncomplicated days when playing football was all about fun and mateship. In my mind, I was Karl-Heinz Rumenigger (West German striker) as my friends and I tore around the paddock pretending we were the world football stars of the day. It seems like yesterday, and now it's your turn.

I can't imagine my life without football. This roller-coaster ride has given me a hobby, a job, a passion, a living and too many opportunities to mention. It has allowed me to travel, taste different foods, smell different smells and meet people from all walks of life, many of whom have touched me in some way. Sometimes it has allowed me to inspire and to be inspired. It has been, and continues to be, an education in life. For all that I am grateful. 'Megs' is a way of sharing my experience and all the happiness that football brought me as a young boy dreaming of football glory.

When I was fifteen someone asked me what I was going to be when I grew up. Naturally I said I was going to be a professional footballer. The next question was 'What happens if that doesn't work out?'. But in my mind, that was a wasted question – I was always going to make it, no matter what! With experience, I now think that a back-up plan would have been a wise thing to have. I also wish I had been a better student and had read more. Like me back then, my young son Julian is football crazy, and he would much rather be kicking a football than reading a book. However, I've realised that he will read anything to do with football – and that is why Megs has become so important to me. If this story encourages kids anywhere in the world to love reading as well as love the game, then Megs will have been a success.

And I hope that Megs will inspire you to dream. Because in the face of doubt and difficulty – discipline, dedication and hard work can make your dreams come true.

Mark Schwarzer

Contents

Some Stuff You Should Know

Nutmeg:

The hard, aromatic seed of the fruit of an East Indian tree, *Myristica fragrans*, used in grated form as a spice.

But more importantly...

In football, and particularly with British football followers, 'nutmeg' refers to a cheeky trick where the person in possession pushes the ball through an opponent's legs and collects it again. This is sometimes called a 'megs' or a 'nuts'. The origin of the name is not confirmed, but here are some interesting suggestions:

Rhyming slang

Like *dead horse* for 'sauce' or *frog and toad* for 'road', some say nutmegs means 'through the legs'.

Shaky movements

When consumed in large quantities, nutmeg can be a stimulant, causing nervous shaking of the limbs and jerky movement. The football trick is said to have the same effect.

Phillip Lunch

In the 1940s, Swindon Town striker Phillip Lunch used to eat several whole nutmegs before games, which would make his behaviour during play eccentric and unpredictable to the opposition. The ball through the legs became one of his better-known trademarks – hence the name.

Bull's testicles

Years ago, nutmeg was used as a spice in the preparation of bull's testicles when served as a table delicacy. The testicles were removed from bull calves to make them steers. Thus the story goes that when a defender was 'burned' by a ball passed between the legs, all you had to add was nutmeg.

Plain old testicles

Some people refer jokingly to testicles as 'nutmegs' due to their wrinkled appearance. Shouting 'Nutmegs!' when doing the football trick warned players that having the football between their legs was like having an extra testicle.

Nutcracker

A nutmeg is a hard, round nut. To crack it, you need to put it between the legs of a nutcracker.

Any more?

If you've heard of any other explanations of this bizarre name for a fantastic football trick, email Megs at: megs@megsmorrison.com

Vootball:

If you've never heard of 'vootball', you'd better read on quick smart!

One | The Final Whistle

The sun had finally begun to peek through the clouds by the time Megs and his dad reached the football ground, but the wind was still howling. Rugged up against northern England's late winter weather, Megs was still surprised how cold his face felt when he got out of the car – even with the club's winter jacket zipped high and his club beanie pulled low. The night's rain had left the pitch sodden and even icy in patches, but the game would still be on. 'It takes a referee with a heart colder than the weather to stop a kids' football match,' Megs's dad had said to Mr Wilson at the end of the party last night. 'These kids would be happy to play in Antarctica!'

Megs enjoyed having people over to his place, and he loved it when the whole family got together as well. He didn't have any brothers or sisters, but with friends and family like his, he never felt alone. Though he did wish they hadn't all been there last night. He wished he could've just watched some football DVDs like he always did before a game instead of pretending to be having a good time.

'So, are you looking forward to it?' Woody's mum had asked Megs.

'Yeah, I think we're ready for it. St Leonard's are a good team, but they aren't great, and we have a lot to play for. We could be champions tomo–'

'No, I mean going to Australia,' she interrupted. 'Are you looking forward to moving to the other side of the world?'

Megs wished people would stop asking him that. If he had a choice, he would leave what he knew about Australia to *Home and Away* and *Neighbours* on the telly. No, he was not looking forward to moving to the other side of the world.

'Yeah. Should be good.' It was his standard response, and he was getting pretty good at it, too. Truth was, he didn't know anything about Australia except that it was a long way away, it was sunny, there were kangaroos, his friends weren't there, and they called football 'soccer'. What was there to look forward to about that?

Of course, his mum and dad thought differently. They kept telling him that his dad just couldn't turn down the opportunity for such a great job in such a great place. Megs thought that his dad was more excited about it than his mum, but the thought had crossed his mind that maybe his dad was just better at pretending than his mum. Whatever the case, they were going to Australia the day after tomorrow, and that was why

Megs's night-before-a-big-match routine had been changed by having all those people at his house. The family needed to say goodbye.

But enough of those thoughts.

There was the Liverpool Regional Under-11 Championship to be won today, and Megs wanted his last game with the Wanderers to be the best ever. He wanted this to be the *real* farewell party.

A smile crept across his face as he and his dad walked hunched against the wind and made it to the pavilion where his team-mates were gathering.

'Hey Megs, how ya feeling?'

'Pretty good, Jacko,' Megs replied with a shiver.

'Bit cold, huh?' said Woody.

'Hope you guys got some sleep last night.' Dan sounded grumpy. 'Billy's and my parents had the music up for *ages* after we left your place. We couldn't sleep until they went to bed at one am! And the place was a mess this morning, too!'

Megs laughed. 'I know. They get well embarrassing when they're together, don't they?'

'How is it that we're the quiet ones when they're all around?' asked Billy.

From tomorrow, Megs would have to leave all of this fun behind and go to live in a foreign country. Without friends, and as far as he knew, without football, either.

It was the coach, Mr McDonald, who brought Megs's depressing bout of daydreaming to an end.

'Righto, kids! Get yourselves inside, out of the cold and start getting changed. I'll be with you in a minute to go through the team. And besides, your little voices are giving us all headaches!'

Mr McDonald had been a professional player with Tranmere Rovers in the second division and was born and bred in Liverpool. He had even played twice for the mighty Reds, and that was enough to win him instant respect from Megs. (That, and the fact that he now worked as a salesman with a lolly company and brought them samples to eat after every game.)

Megs was a central midfielder with plenty of skill and a good football brain. He used to play up front, but Mr Mac thought he could make a better midfielder out of him, and he was right. Megs loved being involved all over the field, and found that setting up goals was just as good as scoring them. Well, almost, anyway. He was one of the stars of the team, and had played every match this season.

The boys made their way into the change rooms to see their crisp yellow and black uniforms hung up around the room in order by numbers. Their shorts and socks were folded neatly underneath, and every one of them had a black towel folded next to their clothes as well. Mr Mac thought it made a big difference to a player's confidence when they were treated well, and he did everything as professionally as possible for his outstanding Under-11 team. He even insisted that every player's boots were spotless before each game and it seemed an essential part of the weekly pre-match speech to say to at least one team-member, 'How can you be a player if you don't look like a player and feel like a player? Go and clean your boots right now!'

Megs couldn't really see the point of all that cleaning when they were about to run around in the mud and would soon be filthy anyway. But the coach was the coach after all, and Megs's boots were as clean as new.

Five minutes later, the coach entered. 'All right, boys, take a seat.' There were never any parents allowed in the change rooms at this point. From here on, the boys were a team alone, and the only people in that room were those who had an effect on the game. Parents did not matter, teachers did not matter, and neither did 'telly-vision', 'that music' or the 'inter-web-net', as Mr Mac kept calling them.

'So it comes down to this,' he began. 'We beat this team and we'll be champions. If we lose or draw and West Docks wins, then we'll come second. So it's up to you. You lot've been the best team this year, and I think you deserve to be champions. But football can be cruel, and what *should* happen doesn't always work out that way. In the end, only you people in this room can make any difference to that – from the eleven that start the game to the ones on the bench. You are a team, and together you can win the championship for each other!'

Some kids had left Wendesley Wanderers because

their parents thought Mr McDonald was too serious and didn't allow enough fun. Sometimes Megs could see their point, but Mr Mac knew his stuff, and the fact was, Megs wouldn't have had such a good season if it wasn't for him. He also knew that Mr Mac wasn't the type of guy who would want to talk about the emotion of it being Megs's last game before going to Australia, and he liked him for that. Leaving the Wanderers, leaving Liverpool and leaving England was basically all Megs had been thinking about for the last month, but right now he didn't want to think about anything – including winning or losing the championship. He just wanted to play football.

By the time the Wanderers had trudged off the pitch at the end of the game, the sun had well and truly retreated behind heavy clouds and pelting rain. The proud black and yellow uniforms were now a sodden mess of brown, and faces were almost unrecognisable. Perhaps the mud would not have smelled so bad if they had won, but they hadn't, so it totally stank. A nil-all draw to finish the season and to send Megs on his way. Coffee-and-tea-carrying parents came to the boys to offer a hug and a smile, but the boys were shattered and felt just as bad as they looked. Hugs just wouldn't cut it.

Mr Mac offered grudging congratulations to the opposing coach, but in truth he also felt just like the boys looked. He was only happy when he won, and with their rivals West Dock playing the worst team in the league, it looked as if the title would slip from their grasp.

'There's still a chance, Megs,' said Mr Morrison, trying to console his son. 'It's not nearly time to quit.'

'There's nothing more we can do, Dad. We've blown it,' sighed Megs.

'Well, you've had a good season and learnt a –'

Dan's dad ran shouting into the change rooms. 'ONE ALL!! Somers Street held West Dock! Can you believe it! They hadn't got a point all season until now! I just rang someone at their game – they drew one–one!'

'Are you kidding? What does that mean for us?' Mr Morrison's voice was incredulous.

'What does that mean? What does that mean? It means we're champions! *Boys – we're champions!*' Dan's dad exclaimed, waving his mobile phone above his head and doing a ridiculous Irish jig.

Megs turned sharply to his dad, eyes bright in his muddy mask as the reality of this news soaked in. A huge smile spread across the older Morrison's face, followed by a chuckle, then a laugh, and a massive bear-hug for his grubby son. Megs laughed too, and whooped with delight.

The next thing he knew though, a chunk of sloppy mud slapped into the back of his head and trickled slowly (and coldly) down his back. He turned to see another clod of earth fly past his nose and collect his father square in the chest. Their laughter turned to shock in an instant, before grins spread across their faces once more. 'Well, that's enough of that, my son,' said Mr Morrison with mock sincerity. 'Let's get 'em!'

Megs's last action as a Wendesley player and champion was a spontaneous, all-in, no-rules mud fight with players, parents and Mr Mac. By the end they were all covered from head to toe in mud, and quite a sight to see, but it was a better celebration than any championship trophy could ever have been. Megs could not have been happier.

Two | The Other Side of the Planet

Seeing the red and white flying kangaroo on the tail of the enormous plane was another reminder of how far away he was going. An expedition to the other side of the planet, and to the only place where the real version of those weird, bouncing animals existed.

He felt pretty good for most of the long flight though, and the thrill of the championship the day before had made anything seem possible. Exciting, even. He felt invincible, zooming across the world higher than a bird – like a real-life action-adventure hero ready to take on all corners of the world.

The Morrisons were adventurous and had travelled a lot for holidays. Megs pretty much always enjoyed going away with his mum and dad (being 'King of the Day' in Disneyland, and skiing in Austria were highlights), but there was an inescapable reality to this trip that made it different.

By the time they finally descended into Sydney, Megs's enthusiasm for the adventure began dissolving.

The in-flight entertainment system began playing a song called *I Still Call Australia Home*, and the lyrics ate away Megs's previous excitement. He no longer lived in England, and now, he was going to have to call a new place home. Butterflies suddenly began zipping around in his stomach. This trip was big. Important big.

As they collected their many pieces of luggage, he felt even smaller. Other times and other airports were for holidays, but you didn't need this much stuff for holidays. This was no fun get-a-way. This was a life sentence!

Then he realised something else. Those pesky butterflies hadn't returned just because he had left his friends and school behind... it was leaving his beloved football that was causing him the most problems. His life until now had revolved around playing, watching, practising and talking about the game. His dad had kept trying to cheer him up over the last few weeks by reminding him, 'Australia beat England three–one a couple of years ago, you know, and they did pretty well at the 2006 World Cup. So some people must play the game over there, mustn't they? And think what it'll be like to play without mud and ice – I know what I'd prefer!' But even so Megs couldn't shake the feeling that football was a thing of the past.

His dad may have had a point, but as far as Megs was concerned, Australia was still a football lightweight compared to England. Sure, he knew about Harry Kewell playing for his beloved 'Reds' and some other

Australian players in the English Premier League – and maybe even one or two in Italy – but in Australia they played cricket, they surfed, they played rugby and that weird Aussie Rules game on a massive field with what looked like fifty-two players on each team. One thing was for sure, he had no plans to go anywhere near the ocean and all those sharks! And he definitely wouldn't be calling football 'soccer' like they did Down Under. That just wouldn't be right.

That said, it was a beautiful March day in Sydney when the Morrisons took their first steps into the sunlight outside the airport. Not a breath of wind, not a trace of clouds, and around twenty-six degrees. Mr Morrison managed to spin around among the crowds (even pushing their life's belongings on a trolley) and screech, 'See what I mean! We're going to *love* it here!' Megs's mum returned his dad's goofy smile, but Megs shrunk behind his trolley and tried to look away from everyone's stares. New country or old, the guy could really be embarrassing at times.

'Graham!' a voice called from across the roadway. A tall man was waving wildly and looking like a bit of a lunatic. *So dad isn't the only one who can be an idiot in public*, thought Megs.

Mr Morrison stopped his spinning when he heard his name, and called back, 'Ahhh, Vincent... good to see you. Thanks for coming to get us.'

'No problems, no problems at all,' grinned Vincent, crossing the road between buses and taxis. 'Did you have a good flight?' Without waiting for an answer, he went on, 'So this must be the family I've heard all about. Hello, Jenny. Welcome to sunny Australia. And this must be Edward... good to meet you.' Cheerfully he shook Megs's hand.

Mrs Morrison smiled at Vincent with an upbeat toss of her head, but 'Hi-ya,' was all Megs managed to mumble. A wave of tiredness had come over him, and he wasn't in the mood to even pretend he was cheery. He was also unused to being called by his real name, and took an instant dislike to this man's slicked-back hair and over-shiny shoes.

Mr Morrison spoke up quickly. 'Jenny, Megs... Edward... this is Vincent Braithwaite – my new boss. He'll take us to our new house.' He turned to Vincent. 'You're from England too, aren't you, Vincent? And quite a football fan...'

'Ahhh yes, but I haven't been to a game for years now,' replied Vincent, looking at Megs. 'I used to watch Chelsea at Stamford Bridge every weekend, but not any more.' He gestured towards the carpark. 'Shall we?' and he led the Morrisons off into their new Australian lives.

Sydney was bigger than Megs had imagined. As they drove through it, he realised that he used to think of Australia as just a collection of small towns on the beach – but the reality that he was now seeing was completely different. So many skyscrapers, cars, bikes, traffic lights and busy-looking people doing busy-looking things. More grey concrete than sandy beaches, but also more sunshine than he'd seen in a lifetime. Megs and his mum, in the back seat of the car, were squinting out opposite windows, taking in the new surroundings, as Mr Morrison chatted with Vincent in the front.

'So, you must be tired, Graham. Such a long flight.'

'Not too bad, actually. I think we're all too excited to be tired,' replied Mr Morrison.

Megs yawned in the back seat. *Speak for yourself, Dad,* he thought.

'Well, that's good news because I have some very important customers I want you to meet in the morning,' said Vincent. 'No rest for the wicked out here!'

'Sounds good. No point waiting around for the action to begin, huh. Best to jump into the deep end, I always say. At least that way you won't hit your head on the bottom!'

Megs and his mum shot each other a quick, knowing glance in the back seat. Mr Morrison's inspirational, positive comments were a running family joke and usually finished up with them telling him what a poet he was. But they held their tongues this time.

By now the car was approaching Sydney Harbour, as Vincent continued chatting enthusiastically from the driver's seat. 'I've come a bit of a long way round to show you what Sydney is all about. People come from all over the world to see the harbour, so I might as well show it off to you now. We'll head over the bridge, then out to your new place.'

The Morrisons were impressed – even grumpy, tired Megs. You couldn't help but be. No wonder so many tourists came here. The Sydney Harbour Bridge stretched out in front of the car in a mesh of crisscrossed grey metal. It rose high above the glistening blue of the bay, and the lazy white sails of the boats below. In the near distance the sails seemed to continue on land in the design of the weirdly shaped Opera House, and behind that, the city rose up high against the blue sky. On the opposite side of the harbour, the bay's jagged edges were dotted with apartments and grand looking houses. Megs saw swimming pools everywhere – even though they were so close to the glimmering bay.

'You'll probably recognise this from the 2000 Olympics,' commented Vincent. 'The city really turned it on back then. All the fireworks around here were incredible. And of course all the tourist brochures and TV shows about Australia inevitably feature the harbour. It's our Eiffel Tower and Statue of Liberty, rolled into one!' Megs didn't know what 'inevitably' meant, but he could tell his dad's new boss was pretty proud, and from what Megs was seeing, it was fair enough, too.

'Wow!' exclaimed Mr Morrison, turning to his wife. 'Can you believe it, honey? This is our new home!'

She nodded enthusiastically. 'I've seen all the pictures, but they don't do this justice. If only our parents could see us now, hey, Graham!'

It felt good for Megs to see his parents so happy, and he noticed the butterflies inside him starting to float away. He was finding it more and more difficult to be tired and grumpy under such a big, blue sky, even though his dad's new boss did his best to bring him back down after they were over the Bridge.

'So, Edward,' he said, 'you're a Liverpool man, I'm told. Seems my boys at Chelsea have had it over you for the last few years. The tide has turned, huh?'

'Well,' replied Megs edgily, 'if we'd spent as many millions as you on players, we'd have won as many trophies. And we've still won more trophies than you over the years anyway.'

'You take this game seriously, I see,' commented Vincent amiably.

'He sure does.' Megs's dad intervened hastily. 'His team won the Liverpool championships the other day. Actually, I think it was just yesterday … I can't tell after being on a plane so long and coming to a new time zone!' Everyone laughed.

Finally, the car turned down another street, and came to a stop outside 20 Valletta Avenue, Pennendale. They were about thirty minutes west of the city near Parramatta, and about one hour away from the sharks at the beach. It was a long street that finished in a court just like Ramsey Street in *Neighbours*. It seemed quiet and spacious to Megs, and there was plenty of grass around the red-brick homes. It seemed that terrace housing was a thing of the past. A thing of their old life.

'So what do you think, Megs?' Mrs Morrison asked her son when they were inside and Vincent had finally left.

'Not bad,' said Megs with a shrug, although secretly he was pretty impressed. 'It looks more like *Neighbours* than *Home and Away*, though. I can't see the beach.'

'*Not bad!*' exclaimed his mum. 'Is that all? I admit the carpet is pretty old and the wallpaper is horrible, but look at all the space! And you don't like the beach anyway…'

'Yeah, okay. It's pretty good,' Megs admitted, grudgingly.

But there was no keeping a lid on Mr Morrison's enthusiasm. 'Oh, it's better than that, Megs. You're really going to love it here – I can just tell! All this space to run around in, and all this fresh air!'

The house already had furniture in it, and it was strange for Megs to walk through his own house with the feeling that it was someone else's. He kept expecting someone to jump out of one of the rooms calling for the police and swinging a baseball bat!

There was a strong smell of mothballs in the air, and the red and gold floral wallpaper was everywhere Megs turned. His room was all the way down the long, carpeted hallway past his mum and dad's room, the TV room, the kitchen, the lounge room, the study and the bathroom. It was almost like Megs had one half of the house, and his parents the other. That much he could handle! In all, there were two bedrooms, two bathrooms, a study, a massive kitchen, a dining room, TV room, lounge room and greeny-brown grass all around the outside. Oh, and a patio area out the back with a ginormous, shiny Aussie barbecue.

'Once we get some pictures on the walls and our clothes and things unpacked, I think it'll be great,' said his mum cheerfully.

'Can we get a dog?' Megs didn't know where that question came from. He had never wanted a dog before.

'Maybe…' said his dad, uncertainly.

'Cool!'

The boxes containing all their stuff had been sent over before they left the UK. As Megs wandered around the house exploring, he could see that each labelled box had already been placed in more or less the correct area. All at once he was eager to start unpacking his things and hurried towards his own room. The room he found was twice as big as his old one, but it seemed cold and empty. Suddenly, he felt very lonely. *Activity is the cure for loneliness…* Megs remembered laughing with his mum as his upbeat dad said this on more than one occasion, but today Megs decided to act on that advice. He started ripping open a few boxes, and in the top of the third one he found some of his favourite posters. He stuck them on the wall and immediately began to feel better.

David Beckham celebrating with the English fans after they beat Greece to qualify for the 2002 World Cup; Ronaldinho, the smiling magician for Brazil; Zidane, the French legend and World Cup winner, and an England team photo from the 1966 World Cup victory. And then the really important ones... Steven Gerrard fiercely tackling Thierry Henry; Steven Gerrard passing; Steven Gerrard scoring for England; Steven Gerrard jumping to head a corner in a crowded penalty area; Steven Gerrard celebrating with fans in a sea of Liverpool red after the incredible 2005 Champions' League victory over Milan; Steven Gerrard holding the 2006 FA Cup... and his all-time favourite of Steven Gerrard with a determined expression on his face, pulling up a captain's muddy armband in the driving rain at Anfield.

'Well, Steve, this is it, I guess,' Megs said to the final poster and to no one in particular. 'My new home. I guess it'll be okay, but I'll sure miss watching you.' He lay on the unmade bed to consider his new room, but with the comfort of some familiar sights now around him, found he couldn't fight off sleep any longer.

By the time Megs woke it was dark, but his grogginess was quickly replaced by a rising panic. *Where the hell am I? What's going on?* He flung himself off the bed as if it was filled with hot coals... and crashed straight into the bedroom wall.

The surprising (and painful) thud quickly reminded Megs where he was. His bed had been on the other side of the room in England, and that was only yesterday.

Today, things were all different, but old habits die hard. Getting out of bed on the 'wrong side' was not the only thing he would have to get used to in this new country.

Anxiously, he fiddled around in the dark for the light switch, then looked around, getting his bearings. He saw that someone had stacked his bedclothes and doona cover on the end of the bed. Some fresh clothes were laid out over his chair, and he could smell some interesting aromas coming from the kitchen. Instantly hungry, Megs smiled as he headed down the passage.

Three | A New Life

'Everyone, this is Edward Morrison. He's just moved here from England, and he'll be joining this class. Please make him very welcome, and show him where things are. Welcome, Edward.'

Miss Sheather seemed friendly, thought Edward, as he stood beside his new Grade 5 teacher at Pennendale Primary School. But still he remained rooted to the spot at the front of the classroom.

'Take a seat, Edward,' she continued pleasantly.

The twenty-five pairs of eyes in the classroom seemed to focus on Megs as he stood clutching his bag, paralysed with fear. *Which seat? Where?* he thought to himself with increasing panic. Every second he stood there seemed an eternity and he felt himself falling into a deep hole of embarrassment. He had been nervous all morning waiting in the reception area with his mum and then meeting the deputy-principal, but now he was all alone, standing like a garden gnome.

'How about over there next to Lin?' suggested Miss

Sheather kindly. Relieved, Megs stumbled forward. He was happy to move away from those staring eyes. He got the impression that Lin wasn't too happy about it, though.

Throughout the first class, Megs was aware of the other kids sneaking secret glances at him. *What's their problem?* he wondered. *It's not as though I've come from Mars.* But he knew that he looked different. He was pale-skinned and short, and his uniform was too new, too crisp and too blue. Although he could see kids from all kinds of different countries, they all seemed to be tanned and casual and somehow made the uniform look so cool. He tried sitting up straight and he tried slouching. He tried chewing on his pen, and he tried leaning forward on an elbow. Anything to look more like his new classmates, but nothing worked.

The first couple of lessons were something to do with fractions, but Megs was just relieved to get through them without collapsing in a quivering heap on his new classroom floor.

'What doesn't kill you makes you stronger' was another one of his dad's motivational favourites. *We'll see if you're right,* Megs thought as the bell went for their first break. Lin got up from her seat and didn't even look at Megs, let alone talk to him, as she raced outside. Some other kids gave him a friendly glance as they bustled past, but no one said a word. Miss Sheather came to the rescue again. 'Edward, the other children will look after you at lunchtimes, and if you need to know anything, feel free to ask them. They'll do their best to help you settle.' The other kids continued to flow past. 'But first, could you go to the principal's office,' Miss Sheather continued. 'He wants to say hi and welcome you to the school.' 'Edward' was pleased to have something to do, so he grabbed his apple and apricot bar and headed to the main building.

The principal's name was Mr Jackson – Megs knew that from the sign outside his office. You couldn't miss it, and you couldn't miss Mr Jackson. He was a big, big man who towered over Megs and struggled to fit on the seat behind his desk. In fact, the buttons on his off-white shirt were straining to bursting point around his ample stomach. Megs tried very hard to understand what Mr Jackson was saying, but he sounded exactly like the Crocodile Hunter on TV and Megs could only understand about every third word the principal said. Megs knew they spoke English in Australia, but sometimes he wasn't quite sure. He left Mr Jackson's office slightly confused, but also – because of Mr Jackson's big encouraging grin – a tiny bit more comfortable about being at his new school.

By the time he was back outside, Megs saw plenty of kids playing, talking, laughing and having fun, but he was suddenly too shy to approach anyone from his class like Miss Sheather suggested. Immediately, he missed his own friends. As a distraction, he pulled his iPod from his bag, found an unoccupied corner of the schoolground, and sat down.

Some of his new classmates shot him welcoming glances and polite smiles as they walked by, but with his iPod blaring, and overcome with nerves, Megs only returned their friendliness with shy smiles, and remained in his own little world.

A horrible feeling of loneliness began to grow, and tears were beginning to well in Megs's eyes, so he decided to keep busy and take a look around the school. He got up and wandered around – still too shy to speak to anyone but again happy to have something to do. The school had lots more grass than his one back in England, and the red bricks in the main building looked much newer than the grey old ones back home. Wearing shorts to school was something Megs could quite easily get used to, but he was one of the few kids who wasn't wearing a hat outside.

The main building sat on top of a small hill and was surrounded by colourful flowers. Below was a large square of concrete bordered by benches and four covered paths leading from the corners. Each path had a set of portable classrooms attached, and the one on the left led to his new room. If he sat in the corner where that path joined the square, he could see the full square, and the grassed area slightly further down the hill where hundreds of kids in blue were chasing balls, hitting balls, skipping or simply chasing each other. At the start of the next path, five younger children were arguing over a marbles game. Just to the right of Megs, at one side of the square, was a small stage and some flag poles. It comforted Megs to see the British Union Jack in the top corner of the Australian flag, but he wasn't exactly sure why it was there.

His thoughts were interrupted by the sound of the bell, so he packed up his iPod and wandered the short distance back to his room.

Lin was still in the seat next to Megs, but barely acknowledged his presence, let alone spoke with him. So Megs settled in as Miss Sheather went through a range of exercises on how to add and subtract fractions using the little squares from a block of Cadbury chocolate. Megs was rarely allowed to eat chocolate, so the fact that they were using it to learn maths was just plain outstanding. He was finding it very easy to like his new teacher.

Before he knew it, the lunch break was upon them, and Miss Sheather called Megs to her again. She wanted to explain the current class assignment because Megs was behind, and they'd all be working on it after lunch and throughout the coming weeks. She apologised, because yes, it meant schoolwork during the lunch break, but it was better than spending an hour alone, Megs thought.

The assignment was called 'Around Australia Car Rally' and the idea was that everyone was given $50,000 to spend in the course of a year travelling around Australia. Obviously it wasn't real money, and they didn't actually travel the country, but each person had to plan a route on a map, decide what they needed to buy, then budget as they went. They then had to report on every place they 'visited' by using the internet for research. Miss Sheather was excited about it. 'It's a good way to teach you maths because of the distances, times and spending your money, and it's a great way to teach English because of all the reports and research. And for someone like you – it's a great way to learn about your new home! You can work in groups when you visit certain places, but you'll need to have a look at a map and get started as soon as you can because everyone else has done that already. Then you can go on holidays without even leaving your seat!' She laughed cheerily and then showed Megs where the maps were. He had to admit it sounded like a pretty cool project, and even though it went against his nature, he was happy to get started right away – it would help to fill in his lunchtime.

Australia is huge, and Megs was amazed to see that the distance between Sydney and Melbourne was pretty much the same distance from the bottom of England to the top of Scotland. And that was only a tiny part of the whole country... man, this was going to be some holiday assignment. *Maybe I could buy a private jet for less than $50,000 to get me around this country instead of having to drive,* he wondered.

With ten minutes of lunchtime remaining, he went outside to his spot and unwrapped his lunch. Today it was white bread with cheese, lettuce and tomato, along with a note from his mum, *'Have a good day, honey'*. The minutes passed slowly until it was time to go back to class.

The rest of the afternoon's classes were uneventful, and when the bell went to signal the end of the day, Megs was the first one out. He had told his mum not to come and meet him, so he shoved the headphones back in his ears, put on his favourite song, and relaxed for the first time all day as he walked back to his new home.

His mum was waiting for him when he got there. 'How'd it go, honey? Did you enjoy it?'

Even through his headphones Megs could hear the anxiety in her voice.

'Huh?'

Mrs Morrison leaned over and removed the headphones. With a smile, she repeated, 'How was school? Was it okay?'

Megs longed to let his misery loose, but it didn't seem fair to lob it all onto his mum. 'Yeah, I guess. But it's hard not knowing anyone. Seemed to drag on forever.'

Megs's mum looked at him thoughtfully, then she put on her cheerful face and remained upbeat. 'Well, it was only your first day, so give it some time. You'll be okay. Come in and have a look at what I've done today.'

The house looked great without all the boxes all over the place, and with the family bookshelves, TV and bits and pieces now on show. (Well, no place could look really great while it still had that ridiculous wallpaper, but it was pretty close.) As he looked around, Megs immediately felt better. 'Wow, Mum! You're right. The pictures look really good. It almost feels like home.'

'Come with me. I've got a surprise for you...' Mrs Morrison led her son towards his room. Inside, every box was as Megs had left it, and nothing seemed any different from this morning. 'I thought you should unpack your own things and put them where you want them,' Mrs Morrison said, reading Megs's mind. 'But look under the bed and you might find something!'

Megs bent down and saw a long, thin package wrapped in silver paper. It was light, and hard to the touch, and he had no idea what it was. Confused but excited, he ripped off the paper. Inside he found a pump. It had an attachment for a bike, and a little spiky nozzle for a ball. But it wasn't the greatest of presents, to be honest.

'Thanks, Mum,' Megs said. 'It's great.'

His mum laughed aloud. 'Don't be silly, you missed the note.'

Megs bent down again, and found a note in the ripped paper. It said, *You've chased it here, you've chased it there. Now it's time to look under your chair.* Mrs Morrison loved these kinds of games.

Under the old wooden chair near his red desk with flaking paint, there was a lump of paper that had Australian flags all over it. Megs grabbed it, but couldn't think what it might be. He ripped away the wrapping and was left holding a beautiful, brand-new football. It was so white it shone, and it had big blue stars around it – just like the one that was used when Liverpool won the Champions League in 2005. It was flat, which was why he needed his first present, but Megs was thrilled.

'Thanks, Mum, it's brilliant! You've done well. I'm impressed!' If balls like this were on sale Down Under, maybe Australia wouldn't be so bad after all.

With that, Megs grabbed the pump and went to work inflating his beautiful new ball. Job done, he raced outside to make use of his new front yard, and belt his glistening present against the brick wall of the house… again, and again, and again. He juggled it on his head for a new record of thirty-seven after only twenty minutes, but even after an hour he still hadn't beaten his old record of 234 using all of his body. He weaved through trees, darted past imaginary defenders, and scored imaginary goals against the outside of the house.

It was getting dark by the time Mr Morrison pulled into the driveway in his new company car. He stopped beside Megs who by then was trying to balance the ball on his foot. He could hold it for about ten seconds on his right foot, but was pretty hopeless on his left.

'Hi son, how was your day?'

'Not bad, I guess. But look at this…' Megs put the ball onto his right foot and balanced like a statue.

'Pretty cool! That a new ball I see? How good is playing with a new ball! Here, you'd better give me a go at that.' Mr Morrison closed the car door and took the ball from Megs.

He actually wasn't bad (even in his business shoes), but couldn't beat Megs's best time no matter how hard he tried. 'Come on, it's getting too dark,' he said eventually. 'Let's go in and say hi to your mum. Hopefully there'll be some dinner, too. I'm starving.'

Inside, Mr Morrison was just as impressed as Megs had been at the work his wife had done in the house.

With his parents smiling like that, and with a good kick under his belt, the stress of Megs's first day at school was slowly evaporating.

'Let's get takeaway for dinner,' suggested Mrs Morrison. 'I haven't even thought about cooking.'

'Good idea,' Megs's dad agreed. 'I saw a Thai place around the corner. We've never had Thai food – how about we try that? In for a penny, in for a pound in this new place, huh? Or now we're in Australia, I should say, "in for a cent, in for a dollar", I guess!'

Their good spirits continued over dinner as the family talked about their day. Megs even managed to admit how lonely he felt at school and immediately felt better. His dad had felt exactly the same at work, apparently, and both his mum and dad told him about starting new schools when they were kids. 'It just takes time,' they had both said, and Megs was starting to believe them.

After dinner they tried watching TV but found they had to choose between current events in a strong Australian accent or American gangster shows, so they decided to postpone TV until another day and head for their beds. Megs wasn't exactly looking forward to Day Two at school, but nor was he as petrified as he had been earlier in the afternoon. Under the watchful eyes of Gerrard, Ronaldinho, Beckham and Co. on his walls, and with his Liverpool and England scarves now laid across the bottom of the bed, he slept soundly.

Four | An Unlikely Friend

Back in England, Megs had not quite been the 'life of the party' like his dad, but he had a lot of friends, and had enjoyed spending time with them. But he *knew* them, so it was different. He didn't know anyone at his new school, and he didn't know how to act around them. He was surprised at how shy he had become, because it wasn't really like him.

But he was organised for Day Two. Along with his iPod, he packed the latest *Shoot* soccer magazine that he had brought out with him from England. The minutes wouldn't drag by so slowly when he had his favourite reading to keep him occupied.

As he went to his place in the classroom, a couple of kids said hello to him and a couple of smiles made him feel a bit better. He managed to say hello back, but was aware that his voice sounded different from theirs, so wasn't confident to say much more than that. For the same reason, he didn't answer lots of questions he knew in class. And there was no way he was going to try a 'g'day' just yet, either. He knew it wouldn't come out right, so he gave himself a mental reminder to practise at home first before trying it out in public. At least he'd already done most of the classwork at school in England, so that was a relief.

At recess, he returned to his quiet corner of the schoolgrounds in front of the classrooms, put in his iPod, and sat, watching the other kids running about. Among the mass of kids, he noticed a group playing football. He watched for a few moments, then reluctantly turned his attention to his magazine.

Then, out of the corner of his eye, he saw a flash of light. It was the sun reflecting off a metal bucket. Looking up, he saw that the bucket was being pushed along by a mop, and that the mop was held by a wrinkly old man with broad shoulders and wispy grey-black hair poking out the sides of a green cap like the stuffing out of an old sofa. He wore grey work clothes and had a thin grey moustache and shiny eyes. He was strong looking, but walked with a limp.

Staring at the man, Megs was thrown when he saw his lips move. *Maybe he's saying something to me,* he thought, so he removed his earpieces.

'Hello. You new here?' the old man said. His moustache seemed to have a life of its own.

'Yes,' Megs nodded.

'Yes. I not see you before. You not sit here before,' the old man said. He didn't sound Australian.

'I arrived this week. It's my second day at school,' Megs explained. The old man looked kind.

'Where you from?'

'I'm from Liverpool in England,' Megs replied.

'Ahhhhh. And you like vootball, no?' the man asked, pointing at Megs's magazine.

'Yep. I play all the time. Well, I used to.'

'What, you retired now? Aren't you a bit young for that?' the man grinned through his straggly moustache.

'No, not retired – it's just because I'm in this country now,' Megs explained patiently.

'So, you like Liverpool or Everton? You Red or Blue?' The old man seemed really interested in him.

'Red. Definitely Red. I'm a Liverpool fan. You know about football, huh?' Megs was impressed.

'I know some,' was the short reply.

'Are you a teacher here?' Megs asked.

The old man laughed, flashing a set of irregular teeth. 'I not teacher, I cleaner! I think you must be from Moon, not Liverpool. Teacher – me...!' The man's laughter continued as he turned away without warning to push his mop and bucket to another part of the school.

For some reason, Megs couldn't help but like the weird old man and his toothy grin; he seemed to know football, too. Megs was disappointed by his hasty departure and, alone again, he turned back to his magazine.

Throughout the rest of the morning Grade 5 worked on their 'Around Australia Car Rally' projects. Megs had to catch up, but if he did some work at home, he knew he'd be able to. He worked quietly in the busy hum of the classroom, and was beginning to enjoy his new project. He'd spent $10,000 on an old 4WD and another $5,000 on camping equipment, which left $35,000 for the trip. Surely that'd be enough ... but he hoped he could get away with buying a cheap old car for such a long journey. Miss Sheather had warned Megs that she might have to charge him some mechanical repair fees throughout the project to keep the game realistic. *Well, maybe as I'm the new kid, she'll go easy on me,* Megs thought cheekily.

Megs had already discovered that there were heaps of the things to see and do on the journey, but so much distance to cover. As well as the beaches that everyone around the world knew about, there were sandy deserts, rocky deserts and huge red deserts. There were massive forests, quite a few cities, lots of big sports stadiums and all sorts of weird animals. There were even ski resorts. *They don't show you that on Neighbours!* Megs laughed to himself when he uncovered *that* piece of information! Most of the photos showed landscapes as far as the eye could see without a soul in sight. In a country so big, Megs was beginning to wonder if all the Australians lived in Sydney and Melbourne and left the rest to the animals and the rocks.

But soon it was lunchtime and Megs found himself back in his special spot with his magazine and iPod. He kept half an eye out for the cleaner, and also couldn't help watching those kids playing football – or 'soccer', as he'd overheard a few people call it. One of them was wearing a full, white headscarf and a flowing blue dress, and some of them actually seemed pretty good at the game. And they were all shapes, sizes and colours. After a couple of days in this country, Megs was starting to wonder what a typical 'Australian' looked like!

Megs was happy when lunch was over and he was back to the safety of the classroom and Miss Sheather, but he was even happier when the final bell went. He raced outside, and only paused to give the old cleaner a wave on his way through the gates.

Phew! Another day over.

When Megs got home, though, things really began to pick up.

'Hi, honey,' his mum said. 'How'd you go today? Was it better?'

'I guess,' Megs replied. It *had* been a little bit better, but only because he took his magazine, and because of that weird old man with the funny laugh and even funnier accent.

'Ahhh, you'll be okay, you'll see,' said his mum confidently, but Megs wasn't so sure.

'Now, don't think that this is going to become some sort of habit, but I've got another surprise for you,' she continued happily.

Megs pricked up his ears. Another surprise! Do two gifts in two days make a habit? Whatever it was called, he liked where this was heading.

'A surprise? What is it?' he asked.

'Well, it's something to help you keep in touch with your friends – and help with your homework. What do you think?'

Why can't you just give me a surprise instead of playing these games! is what Megs thought. But he felt a surge of excitement.

'Dunno! Is it a mobile phone?'

'How's that going to help with your homework?' his mother asked.

'Hmmm, I dunno. Why don't you just tell me?' He was getting impatient.

'Well, why don't you go and poke your head into the study?' she suggested.

Megs raced off down the hall, with his mum right behind him – obviously she wanted to see his reaction to the surprise. Megs pushed open the study door, and there it was, all shiny, gleaming and white. A brand new iMac – with printer, scanner, iSight camera and speakers! The whole kit and caboodle.

'Wow, Mum! You can keep this habit up!' Megs said excitedly. 'It's brilliant! Is it on broadband or dial-up? Does it have normal email or MSN? This is the one with the built-in camera. I'll be able to conference with the lads whenever I want! Does it run version X3 or something newer? Got any games on it yet? Does it have any Microsoft prog–'

'Whoaaa, boy! Slow down!' Mrs Morrison laughed. 'I haven't a clue what you're talking about, but I'm glad you're pleased!'

'I've wanted one of these for *ages!*' Megs continued as if his mum hadn't spoken. 'All the lads have computers at home and I was the only one who couldn't email. Wait till I tell 'em all! Is everything set up?' He was still speaking at a million miles an hour.

'I've no idea. It was organised through Dad's work and someone just dropped it off and plugged it in. There're two manuals here if you need them, and here's a brochure from the provider Dad wants to use – does that make sense? Maybe I could give you a hand if you…'

'Don't worry about it, Mum; I'll do it. It'll be easy.' Having his mum 'helping' would only slow him down. She was useless when it came to anything electronic. She couldn't even change channels on the telly after they'd got their new DVD player, and still couldn't send a text on her mobile.

She's a bit like Mr Mac and his 'inter-web-net' back in Liverpool, Megs thought.

'You know, Megs, I'm not completely useless at tech stuff,' protested Mrs Morrison. 'But granted, I don't know much about computers, so I've decided to do a course. I'm thinking about going back to work, but it's been about twelve years, so I'll need to update myself. What do you think?' His mum sounded a bit apprehensive.

'Dunno. Why do you want to work?' Megs wondered why anyone would work if they didn't have to.

'Well, you're old enough not to need me around all the time, and I'd like to do something for myself.

Coming out here seems a good time to start.'

'Hmmm. Makes sense, I guess. I'll be able to give you a hand with the computer.' No problem, he thought, but right now he was itching to set up the new Mac.

'How about I leave you to it, then?' Mrs Morrison said. But there was no reply as Megs busied himself around the new toy. He was in heaven. School, Australia and a lack of football were far from his mind as he got stuck into the task. Pretty soon the internet was connected and the email up and running.

Time to try it out.

Anyone there? Yep, it's me all the way from Oz. FINALLY Mum and Dad have got us a computer at home – it's a brand new iMac and we have the whole thing – scanner, printer, camera and all. It's weird emailing u guys instead of just seeing u, but it's better than nothing! Maybe one day they'll even let me have a mobile!

Let me know if this gets through, then I'll fill u all in.

By the time Megs had keyed in all his friends' email addresses and clicked on 'Send', it was getting dark. Mr Morrison had arrived home and had settled in front of the TV with a beer – apparently tired after another 'brain-busting day' (his words) at work.

After dinner, Megs returned to the new machine, and spent some time surfing the football sites he and his mates used to look at. It was a happy distraction while he waited for that magnificent 'ping' that sounded when email arrived. But the only sound was the TV in the next room, and his heart became heavier with every passing minute.

'Come on, Megs, turn it off. It's ten o'clock. Time for bed.' Mrs Morrison's voice came down the hall.

'Just a few more minutes,' pleaded Megs. 'I'm waiting for email!'

'Well, you can have a look tomorrow. Anyway, it's around lunchtime back there – the boys will all be at school.'

Megs had forgotten that, and instantly felt better. That's why they hadn't replied! He closed the computer down, and went to sit with his dad for a bit.

'I said bed, not TV. Off you go. I'll be along in a minute.' His mum sure had rules.

Megs huffed, then pulled himself grumpily off the couch. 'Night, lad,' his dad said, sipping his beer and grinning cheekily as Megs trudged off to bed.

By the time Megs crawled under the covers and looked at the posters on his walls, he realised he hadn't even touched his ball all day because of the excitement of the computer. And there it was, still glistening in a corner of the room. So he slid out of bed, scampered across the floor, picked it up, and took it back under the covers with him. That 'new ball smell' was still there, and it seemed to waft over him as his eyelids began to get heavy. It had been a busy few days, after all.

He was asleep before his mum came in to tell him to go to sleep, but the ball was still there, tucked under his pale, English elbow.

Five | An Unusual Day

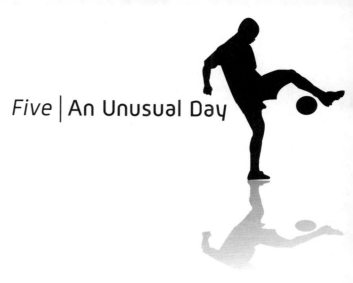

Megs struggled to open his eyes the next morning, and still felt half-asleep after breakfast as he dragged his feet off to school. Even though he had slept well, waking up in a new time zone was taking some getting used to. As he walked out the door, the iPod was back in his ears, and the *Shoot* magazine was in his bag in preparation for the first break. He'd packed the night before.

Then, when he was almost at school, his back suddenly snapped straight. Emails! He'd forgotten to check his emails before he left! He stopped in his tracks just around the corner from the gates, and thought about going home, but knew it would make him late. A battle began in his head …

Maybe, if I run both ways, I can check and still make it in time…

But if there are messages, I'll want to read them and reply – I'll never get back before the bell…

Well, maybe I can just be late and make up some excuse –

they won't care because I'm the new kid…

But what if they do care?

If I just go after recess, it means I won't have to sit around doing nothing in the break…

Anyway, Mum's still at home…

No, she was ready to go shopping when I left…

And that sealed it. Megs turned and walked off purposefully, back the way he had come. He just couldn't resist seeing if his friends had emailed him, and couldn't wait to see what they'd written. He missed them.

Arriving home, he waited outside for a while to see if his mum really had left, and when he was confident enough that she had, he walked tentatively to the back door. He fumbled his key into the lock as his heart pounded in his chest. When he finally pushed the door open and stepped inside, the house felt strange. Different. He couldn't put his finger on it, but maybe it was just because everything was so still. Or probably it was because he wasn't supposed to be here.

Well, he *was* here, and was now past the point of no return. School was just about to start, and he wasn't there. That was now a fact.

He had never done this before.

Down to the computer room he went. He turned the new computer on quickly, his finger shaking with nerves.

Ping, ping, ping, ping… came the sound as Megs logged onto email. Four messages!! All of a sudden, his nerves and guilt were forgotten, and all he felt was excitement.

The first email was from Optus, welcoming Megs to their network. How disappointing. Delete.

The second was from Woody, and *'G'day mate…'* was the title. Megs couldn't help smiling. The next was from Jacko and was titled *'Are you sunburnt yet?'*, and the fourth, *'Check it'*, was from Steve. Dan was the only one who hadn't replied.

Megs opened Woody's first.

Hi ya Megs! It's the first time I've ever got an email from you, weird, huh. But it's cool you finally got a computer at home. Especially now u r over there.

Are you saying 'g'day mate' yet? Do u live near the beach – I guess u do. What's school like? And what about your house? You should take some photos and send them over to us. Mum'd like to see them too. Have you been to Australia Zoo to pat the crocodiles yet? It's been weird not training since the season finished. But what a season, huh – we're going out for McDonalds this Saturday to celebrate the championship. Shame you can't be with us.

See if you can get MSN so we can catch up live with all of us. Or give us a call later – just make sure it's not 1am here or something stupid when you do!
See ya,

Woody

Megs didn't write back, but opened Jacko's email instead.

Hi Megs – good to hear from you! Cool that you're finally online. See what happens when you move to the other side of the world and can't come round to sponge at my place and check the web! Seems a pretty extreme way to get it though – to move so far away. Are all the download speeds the same over there? If you have broadband, you should be able to download the same cool music and check out the same football sites. Better than trying to watch that Australian football, huh. Maybe u can stream some of the Reds games to your PC?

I'm still cleaning mud off me after the game last week. How cool was that! Couldn't believe it when Dad ran full pelt and chucked himself into the biggest mud patch – I reckon he lost his marbles! How cool is winning, huh.

So how's school over there? Do they do the same stuff? Have u been to the beach yet and got sun-burnt? Dad reckons it's a big problem down there and that everyone gets skin cancer. Does anyone play football? The team is going to McDonalds on Saturday for a presentation. Guess you can't come back, huh – I reckon you could get Player of the Year.

What time is it there now, and does it get dark at opposite times, so like 10 in the morning there is actually dark, and midnight is light? Is it like that?

Jack

Jacko had never been very good at geography.

Finally, Megs opened Steve's email, and by now had totally forgotten that he should've been at school.

Steve thought he was some sort of English rap star,

and to be honest, was probably better at that than football, but he still loved the game as much as the rest of them.

> Word Megs. How r ya? R u kickin with some new homies yet, or missin us too much? I'd be missin us seein as we are the best crew goin around. Hopefully Oz is being good t'ya.
>
> It's rainin over here (surprise, surprise) and school still does me head in. I swear Mr Parkinson sets out to get my goat. He's had it in f'me since the very start. He's so wack, man.
>
> You comin back for Macca's on Saturday? I'll eat for ya if not.
>
> Peace out,
>
> Stevie R

Megs had to read this one twice to understand it, but Stevie was Stevie! He sat back in his chair once he was done reading, took a breath, then lurched forward again to start typing. He decided to write one long message and email it to them all at once – including Dan.

> Great to hear from you guys. It's been pretty tough out here, but pretty good in some ways too. Our house is massive and has grass all around it. I've got my own half of the house, and there are heaps of rooms. The wallpaper is DISGUSTING, but overall it's OK. Mum and Dad seem to be loving it. The sun's great and the sky is so big and blue, but no, I've not been sunburnt or got cancer yet. Everything is

spread out, though, and pretty quiet in the suburbs like where we are. The city is great, with water everywhere, but we live a fair way out from there. Haven't been to the beach yet, but I suppose we will soon. Not going in though – too many sharks.

On the flight over I couldn't stop thinking about the game against St Leonards. (Oz is a long way away, by the way, so no I won't be at Macca's on Saturday, Stevie, you pillock) And the mud fight. Being a champion is cool, huh. Keep my medal for me when you get them on the weekend. Don't think I'll get Player of the Year – too many in the running for it.

Haven't seen any football since being here, but Mum bought me a Champions' League ball the other day, so the house wall is getting a workout. Some kids play at school at lunchtime, and some of them look OK, but I haven't joined in. I haven't made any friends yet. I read SHOOT at lunch and listen to my iPod. Can't get used to the weird accents and I reckon I understand about half of what they say. I thought they're supposed to speak English out here! I don't think they understand me too easily either. Everyone looks different, too. There seem to be people from all over the place. It's mostly those kids who play football at school. Wonder where they all come from?

There's a strange old bloke at school that is the cleaner who seems pretty cool. He has a very weird accent and must be about 103 years old, but we speak a bit, and he likes the game.

The work is pretty easy and most of it we've done before, so that's good. The teacher seems pretty cool and I can understand her mostly, but the Head Teacher does sound like Alf from Home and Away! I catch about 1 word in 5!

Football is basically never on the TV, and we don't get any news. Guess the internet will keep me up-to-date, but it's not the same as watching and playing. Guess I just have to get used to it.

And Jacko, 10am is light and midnight is dark just like at home, but it just happens here before it does over there. Don't think too much – it ain't your thing, man!

And while I'm at it – they drive on the same side of the road, they do say 'g'day', I haven't seen Mel Gibson or the Wiggles, or Kylie (unfortunately). I haven't seen Aussie Rules yet, but it seems League and Union are big on the telly and in the papers. Haven't seen anyone surfing yet, and not everyone has long blond hair and muscles.

At that point, Megs heard the phone ring. A little panic set in as he wondered what to do. He couldn't answer it – he wasn't supposed to be there! As he let it ring out, he saw the clock on the monitor had flicked past 10am It hit him that he should've been at school over an hour ago. He'd never missed classes before (except for school sport), and his heart skipped a beat as he thought about how much trouble he'd be in with his parents if they found out.

Gotta go, guys. Should've been at school an hour ago. I'm gonna be in mega trouble if they find out! See ya later,

Megs

He shut the computer down and grabbed his bag. As he left the study and walked towards the back door, he glanced into his bedroom. There lay his Champions' League ball where it had rolled after being under the covers with him all night. It seemed to draw him in, and – his blood pumping with the thrill of already doing the wrong thing, combined with the joy of being in touch with his friends – his confidence was soaring.

Why not? he asked himself, as he stepped towards the ball. Well, there were plenty of reasons why not, but he chose to ignore them. 'In for a cent, in for a dollar!' he said aloud, mimicking his father as he bent over to grab the ball. With it tucked under his arm, Megs made sure everything in the house was how he found it earlier in the morning. He then scurried outside, and, instead of turning left to get to school, he turned right. Within seconds, the ball was at his feet, his bag was on his back and he was all set for a day exploring his new surroundings. In for a cent, in for a dollar indeed.

Before long, he came across a park with plenty of trees, rugby posts and a couple of buildings Megs supposed were changing rooms – but no football goalposts. But at least it was open grass, so he dumped his bag and spent the morning with his football. He used the outside walls of the changing rooms as a kicking partner, swerved past trees and practised tricks in the wide open spaces. At times, he would also rest with the ball as a pillow and stare at the cloudless sky above. Its sheer size unnerved Megs, and added to his feeling of isolation. It was so different from home. Still, he felt lonelier at school than he did here – this wasn't a bad way to spend a day in a foreign land.

After a few hours, Megs decided to explore the streets of his new suburb a bit further. He made sure not to forget the way he had come, though, because the last thing he wanted was to get lost. He had his lunch in the foyer of the local cinema, looked in some shops, then made his way back to the park. He practised some step-overs while dribbling around some trees, and though he still didn't manage to beat his juggling record, he did manage to *finally* flick the ball from the ground up to his head in one move. He'd been trying to do that all his life! This was turning into a great day!

Come three o'clock, his iPod battery had died, and it was time to be heading home anyway. He usually got home at around 3.45pm and he figured he should do the same today.

He timed the return perfectly, stashed his ball securely beneath a bush in the front yard, and walked confidently to the back door. And why shouldn't he be confident? He'd had a great day, and no one would've missed him at school. He preferred the back door as it was closer to his room than the front, but no sooner had it begun to creak open than Megs got the fright of his life. His mother's shriek assaulted his ears as soon as he stepped through the door.

'Where the *hell* have you been? You've had us running around all day looking for you! We've been worried sick! Your father is still out there searching when he should be at work. You'd better have a good explanation for all this – no, you'd better have a MIRACULOUS explanation!!' Mrs Morrison was red in the face and spitting as she yelled. It was the first time Megs had ever seen her like that, and he wasn't exactly sure how to react...

'Ahhhhhh...' was all he could manage as he dropped his bag to the floor and tried to meet his mother's eyes. He could feel his face burning.

'I can't stand to look at you right now!' she continued furiously. 'Go to your room while I ring your father. No! Actually, *you* can ring your father and tell him yourself. Do it now!'

Calling his dad was the last thing on earth Megs wanted to do, but with his mum like this, it was best to just get on with it. He dialled his father's mobile number.

'Hi Dad, it's me...' he began, then his voice dried up, and his mum hanging around was making it worse.

Mr Morrison sounded frantic and exhausted all at once. 'Are you okay? Where are you?'

'I'm at home.'

Then anger overtook relief in his father's voice. 'What the hell have you been *doing* all day? I've had to take the afternoon off to bloody look for you, and your mother has been a nervous wreck! You have some explaining to do, Edward, and you'd better not stuff us around either. I have to go back to work now, but I want you to tell your mother everything, then get her to call me, you hear? You are in serious trouble, my boy.'

With that, Megs's dad slammed down the phone, and Megs was left standing in the kitchen with his father's angry words ringing in his ears. He didn't doubt that he was in serious trouble (particularly after hearing his mild-mannered dad swear like that), and all the fun of his day seemed totally irrelevant. He certainly wasn't about to boast about scooping the ball directly onto his head. But he did wonder how they knew.

'Well?' his mum asked, her hands on her hips, and her angry eyes staring into his.

'Dad's gone back to work, and...' Megs started to reply.

'Not that! What's the story?' It was more an instruction than a question.

Megs could tell his parents were serious – it didn't take a brain surgeon to figure that out – and, faced with a mother so enraged, Megs quickly decided to tell the truth and get it over with as soon as possible.

'Well,' he began tentatively, 'I was waiting to get emails from the guys last night, but, as you said, there's the time difference. So I wanted to check this morning, but I forgot until I got to the school gates.' His talking seemed to be calming his mother down, so he decided to push on. 'So I didn't go into school. I turned around and came home –'

'You *what*?' Mrs Morrison's voice was icy.

'There were messages from Woody, Steve and Jacko, and I – I knew it was wrong, but – but – once I started reading them time slipped away. I meant to get back to school pretty much on time, but then I started writing back to them, and the next thing I knew it was after ten o'clock. I thought I'd go to school then, but I just got my ball instead, and walked around the streets and had a kick in the park.'

Mrs Morrison seemed to become more outraged with every word, and even as Megs was explaining himself, he realised how lame he sounded.

'So you just didn't go to school, and you thought no one would notice? Well, the school had the sense to check on you. They said you've been very subdued, and were kind enough to wonder how we were settling in. They assumed we were out spending the day together. They called my mobile when I was out shopping, and it was then I discovered you weren't at school. We've been worried sick ever since. What *were* you thinking, Edward?'

'Well, no one really knows me at school, so I didn't think they'd miss me. And –' Megs's voice was almost a whisper '– after I'd written back home, I guess I didn't really want to go to this school.'

Megs's mother suddenly sounded very tired. 'Look, we got the computer so we can all keep in touch – but this is home now... You've abused the privileges we've given you. And then to just wander the streets all day – it doesn't bear thinking about. Go to your room now, Edward. We'll talk about this some more when your father gets home. I am very disappointed.'

Megs collected his bag, and walked quickly to his room, glad to be out of the line of fire. He knew he was in real trouble when his parents said they were disappointed. That was way worse than when they yelled and screamed (which didn't happen often, to be honest) but today he had got both! Strangely, though, there was a small piece of him that was happy the school had missed him. At least he wasn't a total non-event in that place.

He sat in his room doing a lot of nothing as time ticked away and was relieved to hear his dad come home at last. He knew he would have to face a punishment, but at least something would be happening and he could get out of his room.

'Edward, come here please,' he heard his mum call. The fact that she used 'Edward' and not 'Megs' meant she still wasn't over being angry.

His mum and dad were waiting in the lounge room. Megs sat down and awaited the firing squad – but it didn't eventuate. Something much trickier began to play out.

'We are very disappointed in you,' began Mr Morrison. 'We thought we could trust you to use the computer responsibly. We thought you understood the importance of school. But to not even turn up for school and just wander the streets in a place you don't know…

I just can't believe it. Do you know how scared you made us and how many people were concerned about you?' Mr Morrison shook his head helplessly as he spoke. 'You almost gave your mother and I heart attacks. What were you thinking?'

Megs sheepishly repeated his story, but this time added a lot more sorries. And he *was* genuinely sorry – he could see how worried his mum and dad were, and was starting to understand why. Then something unexpected happened.

'So what should we do?' his mother asked. 'What do you think the punishment should be?'

This was the first time Megs had ever heard of this tactic, and it threw him a bit. 'What do you mean?' he asked.

'Well, you have to take some responsibility,' his mother continued, 'so I want to know how you think we should punish you. If you think you're old enough to wander the streets and not go to school, then you're old enough to help us work out some solution.'

'Ummm… I don't know…'

'Try to come up with something,' encouraged Mr Morrison calmly.

'Well, I came back to write emails, so maybe I shouldn't be allowed to do that for a bit,' suggested Megs cautiously. Was this a trap?

'Good idea,' said Mrs Morrison. 'For how long?'

'I don't know – a couple of days?' Megs wondered.

'How about a week?' Mr Morrison asked.

'I guess,' Megs replied with a heavy heart. What would the guys think if he didn't send them anything for a week?

'Look, Megs,' said his dad gently, 'we know it's difficult in a new place and at a new school. We miss England too, but we're here now, and we aren't going anywhere, so you'd better start getting used to that or you're going to have a miserable time for years to come.'

'Now get out of our sight before we give you a stricter punishment,' finished his mum.

As Megs trudged off to his room again, he knew his dad was right. But it wasn't easy to just flick a switch and make this new place feel like home.

Six | Giving It a Go

The next day at school, Megs tried to make a point of returning the other kids' smiles and saying hello when someone walked near him in the playground. But his only real conversation was with the old cleaner.

'Hello you,' the old man said, his toothy smile causing his crinkled face to crinkle even more.

'Hi,' Megs replied.

'You not here yesterday. You sick, or you off playing with other kids?'

'No, I was at home.' Well, it was kind of true.

'Sick, no?' the cleaner asked

'Not really. Just didn't come to school,' Megs replied.

'Interesting. So, who is your team – your vootball team?'

Megs was surprised the old man didn't make any more of his 'disappearance' the day before, but was happy to skip over it too.

'Liverpool,' he answered. 'The mighty Reds. I told you before.'

'Ye-es, of cour-se!' was the singsong answer. 'You come from there, yes?'

'Yep. You didn't tell me where you come from, though. Are you Australian?'

'I am Australian, yes, but I come from Hungary. Do you know Hungary?' The old man's moustache danced as he spoke.

Megs was good at geography and he knew where Hungary was, but he didn't know much about it. 'Yes, I know Hungary. It's in Eastern Europe and I think it's a Communist country, isn't it?' Megs didn't really know what Communism was, but he'd sometimes heard 'Eastern Europe' and 'Communism' mentioned in the same sentence and he was trying to impress, so he thought he'd try his luck.

'Ahhhh, not bad,' nodded the old man. 'Yes, it was run by bad men for a while, but that doesn't mean all Communist is bad, yes? Now, Hungary just like the rest of Europe. Do you know the capital city?'

'No,' Megs had to admit.

'Budapest,' the man said as he began to walk off. 'The capital is Budapest. Beautiful. Beautiful.'

'Where are you going?' Megs called. He was not used to someone just walking off in the middle of a conversation. This guy was like a little kid!

There was no reply, so Megs went back to his magazine. He had almost finished it, and would soon have to start looking for something else to keep him busy.

As he turned another page, Megs noticed that four feet in old sneakers had stopped in front of him. He raised his head to see two kids looking down at him – a black-haired boy with big eyes that were almost as dark, and, hanging off his shoulder, a stocky kid with floppy brown hair and a long face.

'Were y' sick yesterday?' asked Blacky.

'Or were y' waggin'?' added Floppy.

Megs forced a big smile. 'Just had some things to do at home.' It sounded weak but the kids nodded.

'Y' didn't miss much,' said Floppy with a grin.

Megs recognised the kids as two of the lunchtime footballers. As he watched them walk away he felt different – as though something heavy had begun to lift off his chest.

Halfway through lunchtime, as Megs watched the Football Kids playing, he felt a tap on his shoulder. It was the cleaner again.

'Why you no play?' he asked, pointing towards the game. 'You play vootball, yes?'

'Yes, I play football. But I don't know those kids,' Megs explained.

'But they just kids like you, no? Bet they love to have you play. What position you like?'

'I'm a midfielder.'

'Ahhhh, the best. The best players are midfielders –

Ballack, Essien, Totti, Kaka, Gerrard, Lampard, Deco … even Aussies Kewell, Cahill, Grella, Bresciano. And what about Ronaldinho! Need to be good at everything for midfield. Hard work, though, no?' There was a glint in the old cleaner's eye as he spoke and Megs didn't try to keep the enthusiasm out of his voice as he replied.

'Gerrard is my favourite, but I like Ronaldinho too. Lampard is good for England, but I hate Chelsea, so I don't like him much.' He enjoyed this old guy's company.

'Which is your favourite team?' he asked.

'Kispest Honved,' replied the cleaner.

'Who?' Megs couldn't work it out.

The cleaner laughed a gritty laugh and continued, 'Kispest Honved is my team in Hungary. In Budapest. They used to be the best. The best. Many great players. You heard of Puskas? Hungary was the best team in the world, you know. In the 1950s they were unbeatable. Even beat England – six–three at Wembley in 1953, then seven–one in Budapest in 1954. First continental team to beat England in England. Much not known about Hungary and Hungary vootball. Shame.'

'Are they good now?' Megs asked

'No,' was the short reply.

'So who do you like now?'

'Kispest Honved.'

'That's it? What about the Premier League?' Megs was intrigued.

'Ahhhh. In England I like Middlesbrough because almost same colours as Honved,' said the cleaner with a grin. 'And in Italy I like Milan because same colours as Honved. In Germany I like Leverkusen, same reason.'

Megs didn't know whether to believe him or not ... surely you couldn't pick a team just because of their colours ... though even he hated every team in blue because of Everton and Chelsea ...

'But Liverpool wear the same colour as Middlesbrough – why didn't you choose them?' Megs asked.

'Ahhhh, everyone likes Liverpool, Man United and now Chelsea because they big clubs. In England, I like club with more challenge. Not always expected to win. More heart. And some Aussies there, too.'

'So, do you watch games here?' Megs asked, keen to learn more about Australian 'soccer'.

'Not much. I come to Australia in 1957, and not play since. I watch some games, but vootball for me is for history and sometimes for TV. Australia not for vootball – Australia for freedom. But getting better, I must say. New competition started 2005, and the Socceroos were good in Germany World Cup too. It was a big deal here. Maybe I go to watch Sydney in A-League, but no-one to go with.'

'What's the A-League?' Megs asked curiously.

'A-League is new competition for Australian vootball. Good crowds too. In NSW, is one team from Sydney, one on Central Coast and one Newcastle. Sydney plays in blue – not like Honved. Your local team in blue – bad luck for you, no!' The old man laughed briefly. 'The others are Melbourne, Queensland, Adelaide, Perth, and even one from New Zealand.'

The old cleaner began to shuffle around with his mop and bucket, an action Megs was learning to recognise as a sign he was about to leave again. So he got another question in quickly.

'When is the season?' he asked.

'Just finished. Wrong time year for you to come Australia! They play in summer, but everyone else play in winter.'

The cleaner then turned to go just as the bell went for the end of lunch. Megs called out one more question to the old man's departing back. 'You said you haven't played since coming to Australia. Who did you play for before?'

'...Kisspp Humnghyyy,' was all Megs could make out from the distant reply.

Did he just say 'Kispest in Hungary', or was Megs hearing things...?

His talk with the old cleaner stuck in Megs's head throughout the afternoon and during his walk home. If he could use the computer at home he could google Kispest Honved and find out more about them, but he dare not go near it after yesterday's episode and the punishment he had given himself. You could still cut the tension in his house with a knife before he had left for school this morning. Maybe he should try the school library tomorrow at lunchtime.

He said hi to his mum when he got home, and munched through an apple and a crumpet. All his recent thinking about football had given him itchy feet, so he grabbed his ball as soon as he'd finished his snack (and put his plate in the dishwasher... you can never be too careful when there's an angry mum around!), and headed outside, determined to break his juggling record.

His first effort was hopeless – eighteen. Next was a more respectable ninety-eight, but still not close to his best of 234.

He tried again, including the 'scoop' straight from the ground to his head that he'd mastered the day before. A couple on his head, then down onto his thighs. You really had to lean back to keep it bouncing on your thighs, but it was worth it because the ball moved quickly and the score could really race up. Down onto his right foot as his legs became tired. Then a couple on his left to take the score to sixty-five, and he was feeling good. Left, right, left, right as he got a good rhythm going, making sure to keep well balanced. Back up onto his thighs to get some quick ones in, and take the total past 100.

Concentrate! he told himself as he kneed the ball onto

his head for five… six… seven more and to give his legs a rest. Back down to his right foot to continue past 110. As he tried too hard to relax, the ball almost got away from him, but he managed to lunge and kick it high in the air, allowing him time to regain composure. He re-controlled it on his thigh because there was less margin for error there, then back down to alternate feet. He wasn't as comfortable on his left, but he'd been practising a lot last season, and Mr Mac had told him how important it is to be able to use both feet well.

The score ticked up towards the magical 200, but Megs was getting tired and was showing less and less control.

One eighty-seven, fin …

One eighty-eight, all good…

But on 189, the ball came more off his lower shin than his foot, and sprayed too far in front for him to re-gather. The ball bounced lazily on the ground in front of him, his personal best would have to remain unbeaten for now.

Megs booted the ball in frustration against the wall. So close, but no joy. As it came back to him, he became aware of someone standing in the street.

Someone clapping and whistling.

Megs spun around to see someone he recognised but didn't know. One of the kids from school. One of the Football Kids. He'd noticed a lot of energy and enthusiasm on the playground, and quite a bit of skill as well. Now, Megs was the one being watched, as the

Football Kid leaned on the fence, holding a bag of DVDs and Playstation games, and looking at him as though he had just walked on water.

'Wow, that was *amazing!* How do you do that? That must be, like, a world record or something!'

Megs took a step towards the spectator but didn't know what to say. But he needn't have worried, because he couldn't get a word in anyway. 'My best is twenty-seven, and you must've just got over 100!'

'One eighty-nine, actually,' Megs said, and immediately felt a bit silly for saying it.

'One eighty-nine! Wow! You'll have to teach me – it's just so *cool*. Do you play? What am I saying – of *course* you play! Why didn't you say so at school?' Then, without waiting for an answer, 'You just sit watching and reading your mag, so we didn't think to ask you – how stupid was that! I mean, not even asking if you played! And we haven't even met properly. Your name is Edward, right?' she asked. 'I'm Paloma.'

'Hi, Paloma. Yeah, I'm Edward, but people –'

'Pleased to meet you, Edward,' Paloma said. She was moving around on the spot so much Megs thought she must have ants in her pants. No wonder she played with such energy, she was practically bouncing even just during a normal conversation. 'So this is your house, huh? I live just down the street in sixty-four. We're neighbours!'

Megs looked where she pointed. 'I guess we are. Have you lived here long?'

'Yep. All my life. Well, I came here from Spain with Mum and Dad when I was two, so we'll call it all my life. Place has changed a bit though. Used to be much quieter. I like it like this though – always something to do. Do you like it?'

'Yeah, it's pretty good.' Megs thought for a moment before adding, 'It's very different from what I'm used to, though.'

'What are you used to? You're from England, right? You have a funny accent,' Paloma said.

'You're the one with the funny accent!' Megs returned with a smile. 'I'm from England where we speak *English*. I'm not sure *what* you speak in Australia!' It was the first little joke he'd made since arriving in Australia, and he was starting to enjoy himself.

Paloma considered this. 'Well, I speak Spanish at home and English everywhere else. Sometimes it's hard to know which one to use!' They both laughed.

'I have to get home, but we'll catch up later, okay?' She picked up her bag. 'Will I see you at school tomorrow?'

'Sure! Why not?' Megs replied.

Paloma walked off, kicking rocks as she went, just like Megs did, and he suddenly called after her, 'Paloma... my name is Edward, like you said, but people call me "Megs". "Edward" sounds weird to me, and it's all I've been called since we arrived.'

Paloma turned around. 'Megs, huh. Well, that sounds

weird to me, but I guess I'll get used to it. See ya, Megs!'

Megs turned back to his ball and his wall. He felt great, and for the first time, he wasn't dreading going to school the next day. Would've been better if she was a football-playing *boy*, but she seemed pretty cool, and from what Megs had seen at lunchtimes, she wasn't a bad footballer, either.

Seven | Things Change

K *nock, knock, knock.*

The Morrisons looked up from their breakfasts in surprise.

Knock, knock.

'Who could that be before 8am?' asked Mr Morrison.

'Well, why don't you get up and find out?' suggested Mrs Morrison.

Megs's dad scraped back his chair and moved to the door. When he opened it, he was surprised to see a young girl about Megs's age. She was a bit taller than his son, with olive skin, dark brown eyes and long, black hair tied in a ponytail. Her schoolbag was enormous.

'Can I help you?' he asked.

'Hi, my name's Paloma and I live up the street at sixty-four. I met Edw – Megs yesterday and I'm on my way to school. Thought he might be ready to go.'

'Well, I don't know. He's pretty hopeless in the mornings!' said Mr Morrison with a smile. 'I'm Graham Morrison. Come on in, and we'll see if we can get him moving.'

Megs had heard all of this, and was busy gulping down the rest of his cereal. Paloma was in his house!

'Hi, Megs!' she said brightly as she followed his dad into the kitchen. 'You ready?'

'Ahhhh ... yep.' Megs leaped up so quickly his chair fell over.

'Hi, pet,' said Mrs Morrison cheerfully to Paloma. 'Just let him brush his teeth, then I think he'll be right, dear.'

How embarrassing! thought Megs. *What is it with parents! Who says 'pet' and 'dear' these days?* He raced off and brushed his teeth in record time, then shot out of the house before his parents could add to his shame with kisses and 'I love you's.'

'I normally get to school a bit early,' chattered Paloma, once they were outside. 'That way I can catch up with everyone before class; after all, it's at least ten hours since my last email! What time do you normally get to school?'

'About a minute before I have to,' Megs replied honestly. 'I don't like hanging around.'

'Well, you can't expect to meet anyone if you do that! You can't have too many friends, y'know!' She turned to him curiously. 'What do you read during the breaks, anyway?'

'*Shoot*. It's a football mag. But I've finished it now. Know it?'

'No. I look up soccer websites and watch games with my dad on TV, but I don't read any magazines. Is it good?'

'Yeah,' Megs replied enthusiastically. 'It's basically about the English Premier League. Nothing on Australia. I'll give it to you, if you like. What games do you watch on TV?' The fact that football matches *were* on TV somewhere in this country had grabbed his attention.

'Premier League, some internationals, and La Liga from Spain – seeing as we're Spanish. My family are all Real Madrid fans. They were fans long before Beckham, Ronaldo, Zidane, Carlos and now van Nistelrooy and Cannavaro came along, and before all the money got thrown around.' There was pride in Paloma's voice.

'Raul is my favourite because he's played for Real for ages and is from Madrid, but my dad keeps going on about Di Stefano and Puskas from when Real won everything there was to win. He reckons they were better than all the current superstars put together.'

Megs had only vaguely heard of Di Stefano and Puskas from TV football shows and the odd magazine – and from the old cleaner just yesterday. He couldn't quite understand how oldies like Pele could be called the 'best players ever' when they played so long ago and most people these days would never've seen them play. He found it difficult to get too excited about those older 'stars', even if it was cool to see the odd bit of black and white footage from years ago. Surely Gerrard would run rings around them...

'It's on Pay TV – it's the only way to see games,' Paloma continued. 'They're usually on really early, though, because they're in Europe. You kinda get used to it. Or sometimes we just record them and watch them later – but it's better watching them live.'

Pay TV, huh, thought Megs. Might not be too smart to ask his parents so soon after the incident with the brand-new computer. But he'd store that information away for later...

'Well... if you don't have your magazine today, you'll have to play soccer instead, won't you?' said Paloma with a grin. 'We don't have a proper school team because no teacher will coach us and Mr Jackson won't let us play otherwise. But the lunchtime games are still pretty good – and it's still soccer, wherever it's played, huh?'

There was no stopping Paloma once she got started – and man, she really did have some energy this early in the morning. Megs got the distinct impression that his life in Australia would never be the same again now that he'd met her.

'I guess you're right,' he said cautiously. 'That'd be cool, actually. But I have a question – why does everyone call it soccer here? It's football.' Megs had been wanting an answer to this question for ages.

'Dunno – but who cares! That's just what it's called – even if I agree with you. In Spain it's called *futbol*, but it's the same game. It's just a name. Just like you want to be called Megs. What does *that* mean, by the way?' She turned to him curiously.

'My friends back home started calling me that because I like to megs people. I've had the nickname for ages now, and everyone just calls me that,' explained Megs.

'What do you mean, "megs people"? I don't get it,' asked Paloma, frowning.

'Y'know – megs,' he explained. 'Nutmegs. Some people call out "nuts" and others say "megs"... and I know which I prefer to be called!' He grinned. He was beginning to enjoy this conversation, even though Paloma was now staring at him blankly.

'Nutmegs? I don't understand. You mean the spice? Don't you cook with nutmeg? I'm sure Mum uses it. What's it got to do with soccer, and why does anyone call out "nuts"?' Paloma sounded genuinely confused. 'They don't mean the nuts you eat, right?'

Megs laughed. 'No, not the nuts you eat.' This girl obviously had a lot to learn. 'When you kick the ball through someone's legs, and then get it again, it's called a nutmeg. I don't know why, but it just is. Look, like this...' Megs then flicked a stone from the path towards Paloma's feet. He timed it so that her feet were at their furthest distance apart as she was walking, and the stone whizzed through the gap, no problems. Megs darted around his 'opponent' to collect the stone again. 'There – a nutmeg! It's my favourite trick.' He straightened up and smiled proudly.

'Cool!' exclaimed Paloma. 'But I wonder why it's called a nutmeg. I'll have to ask Dad what it's called in Spanish,' she thought aloud.

The walk to school was over in a flash, and the next thing Megs knew, Paloma was introducing him to some of her friends. A couple of them were lunchtime Football Kids, and a couple weren't. Megs didn't say much, but it was obvious they were all very happy to be around Paloma.

At the first break, Megs couldn't play with his new friends because he had to go to big Mr Jackson and talk about how school was going and why it was important for him to turn up every day. Megs was surprised he hadn't received this lecture sooner, to be honest, and it was tame compared to the guilt trip his parents had laid on because of his 'day off'. And he certainly had no intention of going through that again! After twenty minutes, Megs left the office suitably told off – but without the chance to enjoy the first recess break he hadn't been dreading.

At lunchtime, he hovered around the spot where he had sat all week, waiting until Paloma came bounding over. 'Here you are, Mr Nutmegs! Ready to play? Come on!'

Ready to play? Megs was bursting at the seams to play!

Eight | More than a Game

There were nine kids hanging about on the patch of grass near the main school building when Paloma and Megs arrived. There were no goalposts, but someone had already organised some bags and clothes into makeshift versions at either end of the patch. They didn't play with goalkeepers, so the posts were quite close together. Some other kids were already playing touch rugby in another section of the playground nearby.

Megs was determined to try and remember names, but it proved a bit difficult when Paloma introduced him.

'Everyone, for those who don't know, this is Megs. Megs, this everyone,' she said.

Everyone – that doesn't help me much! he thought.

'Megs? Did I hear that right?' a dark-skinned boy with chubby cheeks asked from the crowd.

'I thought it was Edward,' another chimed in. He was

a chunky, tall kid with huge feet, and Megs recognised him from class.

'My real name is Edward, but people call me Megs,' he explained shyly.

Paloma grinned at Megs. 'One day he'll explain why!'

'Whatever! Who's got the ball?' said Chubby Cheeks again.

'Weren't you supposed to bring it?' Paloma narrowed her eyes at the speaker.

'No, Jed was. Where is he?'

Just then, everyone turned to see a tall, blond surfer boy come trotting towards them with a ball tucked under his arm. It was old and battered, but it was fairly round, so Megs supposed it would have to do.

'Hi, everyone,' Jed said. 'Sorry I'm late. So, who's captains today?'

'You and Matteo,' Paloma answered, with general agreement from the rest of the Football Kids.

'Right,' said Jed. 'I'll pick first. I'll have Adam. Your turn, Matteo.'

'Ahhh, Biscan,' Matteo said much more quietly than Jed. Megs recognised Matteo as the black-haired, black-eyed boy who had spoken to him the day before. Megs instantly hoped he'd get picked for Matteo's team.

'Ivan,' Jed called immediately.

'Danny,' followed Matteo. Megs recognised Danny as Matteo's 'floppy' friend from the other day. Danny pushed his hand through his hair, and Megs saw a huge smile light up his long face as he walked towards his friend.

'Uhhmmm... Seb,' was Jed's next choice.

'Paloma,' said Matteo.

'Sam.'

Megs was standing nervously with the remaining five kids, each willing themselves to get picked next. No one wanted to be the last one, even if you were among friends. The last among people you were just meeting would be torture. Megs saw Paloma whispering something to Matteo before he turned his eyes back to the grass at his feet.

'Megs,' was the next name called, but at first Megs wasn't sure because of Matteo's soft voice. The murmur passing around the other kids confirmed it was true, though – the new kid had a team.

'Left your reading behind today, huh, Edward-Megs?' Jed commented dryly, then turned to the other captain. 'Hope you know what you're doing, picking a Pom for your team, Matteo. The Simpfenators want a game today!' Megs wasn't sure if Jed was being serious or not, and he had no idea why he said 'the Simpfenators', but he walked over to Paloma and stood silently while the remaining four kids were picked.

Matteo got Angelique and Mitch, and the 'Simpfenators' got Abda and Max.

'What's a "Simpfenator"?' Megs asked Paloma as the two teams moved to either side of the makeshift pitch.

'Ahhh, don't worry about him,' she replied. 'His last name's Simpfendorfer – I think he's German. He's always trying to get people to call him Simpfenator. No one does though... pretty good player,' she added.

'Hi, Megs, I'm Matteo,' said the day's captain. 'You've heard these kids' names – Angelique, Danny, Mitch and Biscan. Biscan just came to school a couple of months before you and he's still learning English. And you know Paloma.'

'Hi, everyone,' Megs said brightly, happy he now had some names to work with. It would certainly help when they got to playing. And that didn't take long.

'Come on, you lot, let's play!' Jed called out as he dropped the ball to his feet and passed wide to Ivan. It was game on.

Matteo's team quickly left their huddle and went about trying to get the battered old ball into their control. Paloma gradually drifted forward to their attacking goal, while Matteo promptly fell back to defend. Megs couldn't help it – he ran straight into the fray among the hustle and bustle to get that ball.

The game began frantically, with the Simpfenators in control. Biscan ran towards Adam to defend as quickly as possible when Jed's team made another break, but Adam took the ball with great skill, and quickly changed direction. Biscan went flying past him, slipping over unceremoniously as he did so. Next, Megs ran in to close down Adam's space. Just as he'd been taught, Megs kept his eye on the ball as he cautiously approached his opponent – not being fooled by his swaying hips and tricky feet. This process slowed Adam right down, so he decided to pass the ball off to another team-mate. Megs had done his job.

The ball was passed to Max, but he didn't even try to control it because Angelique was standing right next to him ready to pounce. Instead, Max just swung his huge foot and tried to get the ball as close to the Simpfenator goal as possible. Unfortunately for him (but to the delight of the other team), he did a complete air-swing, and fell with a thud onto his backside!

The ball flew aimlessly past both the attacker and defender. Jed was the most alert and got to the loose ball first. Matteo was the closest defender, and ran towards the opposing captain. Matteo knew what he was doing, and, as Jed tried to confuse him with a quick change of direction, the quietly spoken defender read it well, and was in the perfect position to stick out his foot and dispossess the opposing captain. The ball rolled up towards Matteo's attacking goal, and towards Paloma in her preferred position up front. Hot on her heels was Seb, but Paloma got to the ball first. She controlled it expertly, but, with her back to goal and with Seb trying desperately to get possession, Megs could see she needed some help.

'Paloma, now! Pass!' Megs called as he darted forward in support.

Paloma didn't even need to look up, and rolled the ball perfectly into Megs's path. He didn't try to control it and, even though he was about fifteen metres out, he knew exactly where the goals were. Without thinking, he let fly. His first touch was the first shot of the match.

The ball sizzled off his right foot towards the two bags that made the goal. With only a metre between them, it was a tough target from such a distance, but Megs's instinctive strike looked destined for glory.

THWA-ACK!!

The ball thumped against the right-hand bag and stopped dead. No goal, and the ball was still in play. Biscan reacted first, and flew towards the ball with Sam in hot pursuit.

'Go on, Biscan!' Paloma cried out, clapping her hands together. Sam's face was grimacing as he strained to keep up, but Biscan's quick thinking had given him the initial lead, and he kept it all the way to the ball. By the time he got there, all that was required was a simple side-footed tap in.

'YE-ESSSS!!!' screamed Paloma as Biscan turned, stood still and posed like a rock star on MTV until his team-mates ran to celebrate with him.

Megs had played his part, and was loving the feeling of playing again, and of being part of a team.

The Simpfenators got on with the game as quickly as possible, and began to put Matteo's team under a lot of pressure. Yet Matteo proved himself time and time again in defence. He always seemed to be in the right place, and could usually find someone to pass to. Mitch didn't have great control on the ball, Megs noticed, but was always around the action, putting opponents off and winning tackles. Danny and Biscan tended to stay wide and use their pace, and Angelique was Matteo's able assistant in defence. She had a great eye for the ball and was superb at clearing the lines, although she didn't like doing headers one little bit.

Despite all that, the Simpfenators managed to score three goals in the next twenty minutes, with good work by the tricky Adam and powerful Seb. Abda was the girl Megs had previously seen from a distance playing in a full headscarf and flowing blue dress. He had never seen anyone so graceful with the ball – it was as if she was dancing every time she moved. Jed was trying to control midfield, and used his physical strength to hustle and bustle Matteo's players. Megs was bumped out of the way on a number of occasions, and it was after the third shove that he realised that maybe – just maybe – people *did* take the game seriously Down Under. He was pleasantly surprised with the standard of the Football Kids, and was really enjoying himself.

After his team conceded the third goal, Megs decided that he was being too polite. He wanted to be liked and didn't want the others to think he was a show-off, but losing 3–1 was losing 3–1. And Megs didn't like losing.

From the kick-off after the third goal, Megs took possession. He faked passing the ball wide left to Danny, just as Ivan came close to defend. He then changed his passing action, twisted his body, and went the other way. Ivan was left stranded, while the ball was perfectly in Megs's control. Next, he found himself running straight at Sam, and just as he had practised it countless times, he stepped over the ball at pace with his left foot, then took the ball with the outside of his right foot, and left another defender for dead. Megs was now powering towards the goal.

Paloma was off to his left, calling for a pass, and Mitch was up in support as he always was. Just as Megs was about to pass the ball over to Paloma in a goal-scoring position, Jed's long strides drew him closer to the new kid from England.

CRRU-UNNCH!

The Simpfenator clumsily ran straight into Megs, leaving him sprawled on the grass. It was a high-paced, physical clash, and the game immediately stopped.

'Relax, man!' said Matteo, raising his voice.

'Take it easy, Jed – he's half your size!' exclaimed Danny.

Paloma and Mitch ran to Megs's side to see if he was all right. Gingerly, he got to his feet and said, 'Yeah, I'm okay. No problems.' He didn't want to make a fuss around his new friends, and he had his own way to pay Jed back.

To his credit, Jed muttered a half-hearted apology once he knew Megs would be okay, and put the ball down for a free kick.

'It should be a penalty, not just a free kick!' said Angelique. 'That's only fair.'

'Yeah, that's right. You were the last defender, and

you just took him out,' agreed Danny, looking at Jed.

'Fair enough,' agreed Abda, 'but you have to take it from there.' She was pointing to a spot about ten metres out, but on a pretty tight angle to the right. It left the one-metre gap between the posts extremely narrow, but, although Megs was shaken by Jed's rough tackle, he still wanted to take the kick. With the ball placed, he approached it confidently, and struck it firmly towards goal.

'WHHOOAAA!' shouted Paloma as the ball headed towards the goal.

It went straight past the right post, scraped the inside of the left post... and trickled in.

'YE-ESSS!' was the collective cry from Matteo's team, followed by high-fives all 'round. As far as Megs was concerned, that was the best way to pay Jed back for the tackle, but not the end of it. He knew how to really bring him back to earth, but – all in good time...

So, the score was 3–2 and there were about five minutes to go before the end of lunchtime. This kick-about had turned into a high pressure game as competitive as a Premier League match!

The Simpfenators attacked again, straight from the kick-off, but couldn't make another breakthrough. Abda, in particular, was gliding into dangerous positions for Jed's team, while Max and Seb were getting very involved.

Because of the Simpfenators' aggressive tactics, every one of their players became crowded around Matteo's goal. With so many players in such a tight space, the game turned into a messy tackle-fest. Paloma, however, decided to stay further up the field and take a risk, seeing that her team was losing and time was running out fast. Many shots just missed Matteo's goal, and Angelique was performing heroics in defence to keep the score at 3–2.

Then the ball somehow squeezed out of the mess of bodies.

Matteo chased it down and just managed to keep it in play. Then he looked up to see Paloma alone by the goal, so he booted the ball with all his might in her direction. It was a wonderful kick, and left the Simpfenators trailing in its wake.

Megs remembered something Mr Mac had said, one particularly cold training night back in Liverpool: 'The ball is faster than the man, Megs. More often than not, it's better to pass.'

The ball reached Paloma with only a couple of bounces, and with no offsides in lunchtime soccer, she had plenty of time by herself to control it, turn, and slot it between the bags for the easiest of goals.

The celebration that followed looked more like something you'd see in the World Cup Finals, than in a school playground at lunchtime!

Moments later, the bell went to mark the end of lunchtime, and therefore the end of the game. There was no winner, but plenty of happy players. It had been a brilliant game.

'That ended up being pretty serious, huh!' said Angelique, as they trooped back to class.

'Thought we had you there!' Abda replied. 'It was good, though, today. The teams were really even. And you did well, Megs.'

'Thanks, Abda,' replied Megs. 'It was fun. Better than sitting in a corner!'

'Well done, man. Should've guessed you Poms could play a bit, huh?' This time it was Max patting Megs on the back with one of his big hands.

'Yeah. Back in England my team won the championship just before I left to come here, but I haven't played since,' Megs replied.

'Told you he was worth it!' It was Paloma's turn to congratulate Megs – and partly congratulate herself for discovering his talents!

By now they had reached the main part of the school, so they split up to head for their various classrooms. Some of the players went the same way as Megs, and others went elsewhere, while separate conversations continued.

Megs was on top of the world. Yeah, he had played okay, but, more than that, he now felt like he was part of the school. He was now one of the Football Kids, and they were calling him Megs.

Nine | When Does the Weekend Finish?

Megs was itching to email his mates back in England, but knew it wasn't worth his life to ask his mum if he could use the internet yet. His week of punishment wasn't up.

'Mum, can I call England?' Megs asked hopefully.

'No, Megs. If I let you do that, it'd make your ban from the email seem pointless, wouldn't it?' his mum replied.

'Come on,' he begged. 'It's not the internet. I just want to tell the lads about my week!'

'Look, I'm not happy about it, but I have to stick to what we said. A deal's a deal.'

'It's not fair!' Megs complained. 'They're gonna wonder what's going on because I haven't emailed them back!'

'Well, the worry you put your father and me through wasn't fair either, was it?' Megs's mum pointed out. 'Look, why don't you tell me about your week? That

Paloma seems nice…'

Megs walked off to his room without another word. Sometimes parents just didn't get it.

Half an hour later, Megs heard Mr Morrison's voice at his bedroom door. 'Come on, Megs, time to go.'

'Go where?' Megs couldn't keep the irritation out of his voice.

'For a drive. Thought we'd all go to the beach and have a look around. No point sitting inside all day when it's so nice outside. You remember my boss, Vincent? Well, he's asked us out, so get yourself sorted, and let's go. He's asked us to meet up at Bondi Beach. Come on – there's Sydney to see!'

His dad's enthusiasm was infectious, and while he wasn't thrilled about seeing his dad's boss again, Megs slowly perked up. Within thirty minutes, the Morrisons had piled into their new car and set off to explore their new home town.

They met the Braithwaite family at the famous Bondi Beach, and marvelled at the people managing to surf those big blue waves – like rock climbers on a moving blue mountain. *I wonder if sharks ever surf?* Megs thought, as his bare feet crunched over the warm sand… at a safe distance from the water's edge.

The Braithwaites weren't as much of a drag as Megs had expected. Spending the day in the company of adults was far from ideal, but as it turned out, Vincent was actually a lot of fun if you just went along with his corny jokes. He also managed to convince Megs's dad that it was okay for a growing boy to eat three ice-creams in one outing, and he went ahead and bought them for Megs each time before Mrs Morrison could even argue. Not only that, he ate just as many himself, and that deserved respect.

Even though Vincent regularly made fun of Megs's beloved Liverpool FC, he actually knew quite a bit about football, and along with Mr Morrison, the three of them talked almost non-stop about the game. In fact, they could've been in England if it wasn't for the backdrop of sun, sea and sand. Meanwhile, Megs's Mum was happily talking to Mrs Braithwaite about working in Australia, and the types of things she should do to help her find a job. The more they talked, the more Mrs Morrison seemed to think a computer course would be a good idea.

They looked at some market stalls that were pretty similar to markets back home, then had a drink at a café. It was so slick and trendy compared to seaside places in England, thought Megs, and there were so many to choose from. Not only that, but Megs didn't understand what most of the things on the menu were, and Vincent had to explain that Australia now had dishes from all over the world, and usually seemed to keep their original names. 'It's not just curry-and-chip suppers for you anymore, young man,' he concluded with a smile.

They walked along the cliffs to another beach, past an old cemetery perched high above the rocks, and loads of fit-looking people raising a sweat as they jogged along under the sun. The sound of seagulls filled the air as lots of people spread out picnics under the big blue sky. The water sparkled in the sun, and the sand was so white it almost looked fake. *I really should get some sunnies,* Megs thought. He had to admit he was enjoying himself even though he wanted to go on being grumpy about not being allowed to contact his mates. And his mum and dad were having a great time – it was a bit embarrassing, really, how they held hands and hugged like teenagers. The fresh air seemed to have gone to their heads. And it was *really* embarrassing when his mum decided to give Megs a hug as well.

'Mum, *don't!*' he complained, wriggling away. 'We're in *public!*' He decided it was safer to walk just out of arms' reach of them to avoid the risk of future embarrassment.

Megs was thrilled when they stopped for fish and chips on the beach. The fancy food in the cafés could wait – give him a fish supper any day.

'Reminds me of home,' remarked Mr Morrison, taking his first chip from the greasy carton, and Megs's mum nodded. It wasn't just Megs who was happy about the day's lunch.

'The seagulls are pretty full on here,' Megs observed as another one jumped right into his remaining chips.

'Maybe Aussies don't feed them properly!' his dad replied as he threw some of his scraps high into the air.

After lunch, they watched some street performers breathing fire and balancing on their heads, then returned to the car for a drive into the city. Megs began to feel the heaviness of sleep come over him as the sun came through the car windows to warm his face. And he wasn't at his best when he was tired.

'What a beautiful place this is,' Mr Morrison said to Mrs Braithwaite for the fifteenth time, as they walked through the old part of Sydney that was called The Rocks. *Pretty boring name,* Megs thought.

'I know – incredible place! And we live here!' Mrs Morrison replied for the fifteenth time. *Pretty boring conversation,* Megs thought.

They walked around Circular Quay and under the Harbour Bridge, then jumped onto an old Sydney ferry to see the Opera House from the water. It was all very spectacular, but Megs was starting to get tired of all the sightseeing. *It's just another view,* he thought. He didn't feel like talking anymore, and his motor-mouthed mum and dad were carrying on enough for the five of them anyway.

On the drive home, Megs began thinking about school – well, not about school exactly, but about the people he had met on Friday during the game. And about the game itself. Amazingly, he was actually looking forward to the weekend finishing so that he could go back to school again. Maybe he should take his Champions League ball with him on Monday…

With the smooth movement of the car, the sun continuing to warm him through the back window, and the happy thoughts in his head, Megs drifted off to sleep.

He woke when the car stopped back at the Morrison house. He groggily opened his door, then spilled out into the front garden, still half-asleep.

'You really like to sleep, huh, Megs!' He heard an unexpected voice, followed by his parents' laughter.

'Hi, Paloma dear. How are you?'

'Good thanks, Mrs Morrison. I just came past to see if Megs wanted to have a kick.'

Paloma must think I'm an idiot! Megs was wide-awake by now.

'Well, I reckon you've come to the right place – that's about all he ever wants to do,' Mr Morrison said with a friendly smile.

'Cool!'

Megs's parents went inside and left the two Football Kids alone.

'Well, come on! Wake up. Time for some *futbol!*' said Paloma, full of enthusiasm – as usual. She threw the ball to Megs, and ran off to another part of the front yard to receive a pass.

'Fair enough,' said Megs, feeling his energy levels rising. 'You need an Englishman to show you how to play this game, anyway!' He had already controlled the ball, and was in the process of belting it into Paloma's path. She stopped it and passed it back very accurately – and very forcefully.

'You don't know anything until you learn from a Spaniard!' she called out.

Megs began darting around the yard, spraying long-distance passes all over the place, just like Gerrard, and Paloma tried to recreate the deft touch and skills of Raul – her favourite player. The two kids continued to joke and play for the next hour, until Mrs Morrison's voice interrupted them.

'Megs, time for dinner!'

Megs shot a glance at the kitchen window, then turned to Paloma. 'Well, looks like game over. Guess I'll see you later, Raul. Thanks for coming over.'

He walked inside, feeling very cheerful – and hungry. He polished off the roast lamb with gusto (it was his favourite meal, just edging out fish & chips), then sat in front of the TV and tried to make some sense of it all. There was a rugby league game on, but he didn't even like watching the game in England, so there was no point giving it any time in his new home either. He flicked over to another channel where they were showing Aussie Rules. *Aerial ping-pong*, Megs had heard it called, or *AFL… footy… football…*

'Do you get this game?' Megs asked his dad after he'd joined him on the couch.

'Not really. Seems pretty simple, though. Big, fit guys running around, bumping into each other.'

'I can't believe they call it football. They use their hands more than their feet!' Megs said.

'True,' his dad laughed. 'Not much skill, but they are pretty tough. Got to give 'em that.'

The two of them watched the entire game, trying to

make head or tail of the rules, though there didn't seem to be many. Once they'd figured out that scoring through the big goals earned six points, and through the small goals only one, the game began to make a bit more sense. The commentators were continually reminding viewers that Sydney was in the 2006 Grand Final and a chance for the 2007 title, so both the Morrison men figured they'd be a good choice for a team to support. The fact that they wore red and white sealed the deal.

The match had a very close, exciting finish, and by the end, the Morrison men found that they were enjoying themselves. A weird game, but kind of exciting.

But Megs wasn't silly, and he saw an opportunity.

'Dad, there's never any real football on TV here. Do you think we'll ever get to see the Reds play again?'

'Not sure, son. They must show some games here, mustn't they?'

'No, I've looked,' Megs said. 'They're shown on another channel. All the Premier League, Spanish League and even the Australian A-League when it starts again.'

'Well, there you go. So it is on,' his dad replied.

'Well, thing is, they're on Pay TV, not normal TV,' Megs said, shifting in his seat.

'Pay TV? Oh, I don't know, Megs. We'll have to think about it later. It's expensive moving to a new country... I'm not saying no, but just no for now,' his dad concluded.

'Fair enough, I guess,' Megs replied reluctantly. He

couldn't really expect any more. At least there was a chance.

'Bedtime, Megs,' came his mum's voice from the study. She sure was good at keeping an eye on the clock.

Megs got up without a fuss, and said goodnight to his dad. His day had actually turned out to be a pretty good one, and he wasn't bothered about hitting the sack – he was exhausted.

The next morning over breakfast, however, Megs wished he *had* made a bit of a fuss about staying up longer. Woody's family had called from England after mistaking the time difference. Megs was not happy about not being woken up to speak to his good friend.

'...but, Megs honey, it was almost midnight when they called. I poked my head into your room, and you were sound asleep,' Mrs Morrison repeated, as she had been doing throughout the morning. 'You've only got a couple more days, and you can be back on the email. You can give him a call then, too.'

'Well, it's not hard to wake me, you know. I didn't have to speak long. It just doesn't seem fair, that's all. You got to speak to them.' Megs couldn't leave the subject alone.

'Well, I didn't just take a day off and wander the streets, either,' his mum said with increasing irritation.

'This is different,' Megs replied. 'I haven't been in touch for almost a week. It's not fair.'

He scooped the rest of his porridge into his mouth, then got up without a word, ignoring his dishes as a small protest, and turned to walk up the hall to his room.

'Megs – come back and put your dish in the dishwasher. It's not hard!' called Mrs Morrison.

Huffily Megs turned, and did what he was told. Except that he left his spoon on the table. That'd show her!

He had homework to do, but he couldn't bring himself to do it. So he spent the morning in his room going through his things, reading old *Shoot* magazines and drawing pictures. As the hours passed, he found himself looking forward to going back to school. He was keen to see Paloma and the Football Kids again, and wanted to know more about that old cleaner. Megs didn't even know the old man's name!

He wondered if they would keep the same teams for the lunchtime game, or change around again. At the very least, he hoped he would be on the opposite team to Jed. He didn't mind the guy, but it was time to show him that just because he was big didn't make him the boss of the game. Megs had some payback to give, and he was going to do it Megs style.

Ten | Watch and Learn

'So, why Megs?' Abda asked as Megs, Matteo, Biscan, Max, Jed and Paloma walked down to the 'football pitch' for the lunchtime game.

'Good question!' Paloma said before Megs could answer. 'How long can he have to explain it?'

'I can't believe you all like football, and have never heard of a megs,' Megs said. 'It comes from "nutmegs". Surely you've heard of nutmegs...'

'I've heard of nutmeg, I think,' said Max, 'but I don't know what it's got to do with soccer.'

'It's something to do with food, isn't it?' asked Abda. 'A spice? You put it in desserts.'

Paloma was chuckling to herself, enjoying the confusion.

'Look,' Megs continued, 'some people say "nuts" and some people say "megs" when you do a nutmeg, so I...'

'*Do* a nutmeg?' interrupted Biscan, still baffled.

'It's a cool trick with the ball,' explained Megs.

But by now the crew from Megs's class had made it to the pitch where the others were waiting. 'Come on, you lot!' called Jed. 'We don't have all day!'

'Look,' said Megs, finishing the conversation with a little grin, 'how about I just show you? You'll know a nutmeg when you see it.'

It was decided that the teams would stay the same as the last game. It had ended 3–3 after all, so they could consider this a kind of extra time.

The match was as evenly contested as the last one, and Jed in particular seemed very keen to make sure his team came away from this lunchtime victorious.

Perfect, Megs thought; he planned to bring the bossy opposing captain down a notch... as well as teach the Football Kids a thing or two about playing the game English style. His old confidence was coming back.

Only a couple of minutes into the match, Megs found himself in possession, out towards the left wing. Biscan was a little further forward and a bit wider, and Jed was bearing down on him with his trademark power. *Perfect,* Megs thought again, as he prepared to teach the Simpfenator a lesson.

Megs could see Jed flying towards him, and knew it would be too difficult for him to change direction, coming in at such a pace. He was sure Jed wanted to put him on his backside again, so Megs shaped to pass wide left to Biscan with his right foot just as Jed was within reach. Immediately, the opposing captain stuck out a long leg to block the pass and rob Megs of possession. But Megs had sucked him in perfectly, and instead of passing, flicked the ball with the outside of his right foot back towards the onrushing defender. The ball scarcely even moved a metre, but that's all it needed. It was enough for the ball to slide in between Jed's outstretched legs as clean as a whistle. Megs skipped past to re-collect the ball, leaving 'the Simpfenator' stranded, red-faced with embarrassment, and with steam coming out of his ears.

'NUTMEGS!!' Paloma shouted with glee as Megs raced off in possession.

Hearing that call fired Megs up, and made him think that he might as well really rub it in. He knew Jed was angry, and Megs had a feeling his efforts to flatten Megs would be redoubled. And sure enough, the big blond midfielder had turned, and was charging after the short Englishman again. With a touch of arrogance, Megs slowed down and drew Jed closer. Paloma was standing off to the left of Megs, and would be the perfect pass. If he was back playing for the Wanderers in a proper match, he would've passed, but he was only in a schoolyard, and for the first time in a while, he was bristling with self-belief. So he shaped to pass, but as Jed stretched out to tackle, Megs once again turned the ball towards the fast-moving defender and slipped it in between his legs. Once more, he skipped around him to re-collect, then immediately passed off to Biscan who had drifted towards the unprotected goal, and was in a great position to finish easily. One–nil.

'NUTMEGS!!' Paloma shouted again, laughing.

Megs couldn't resist a smile. He turned to Abda and said, '*That* was a nutmeg. It's my favourite trick – and that's why people call me Megs.' The lesson was complete, and everyone on the pitch – except Jed – had thoroughly enjoyed it.

But even the Simpfenator could see that what Megs had done was pretty cool, and since everyone on the pitch was laughing and calling out 'NUTMEGS!' or 'MEGS!', he knew that getting angry was pointless.

'Not bad, Megs. I have to give it to you, not bad. Maybe you Poms *can* play a bit... but I'll be looking for it next time,' he concluded, before quickly getting the game started again. So long as there was a game on, no one would be laughing at him.

Throughout the rest of the match, scoring goals became secondary to trying to 'get a meg'. Only Danny managed it, even though the ball only just made it through after bouncing off both of Ivan's ankles. Not a clean nutmeg, but a nutmeg just the same, and Danny was thrilled. 'MEGS!' he called out, himself, after he managed to clumsily re-collect the ball.

The match finished one–nil (or 4–3 if they included the previous day's game), but no one seemed to care. They were having too much fun trying to embarrass each other, and went back up to classes laughing and joking. And Megs was the man of the moment.

'How did you learn that?' Ivan asked. 'It's so cool!'

'Dunno, really,' he replied. 'All my friends would try it,

but I seemed to do it the most. So they gave me the name.'

'I've gotta admit, it's cool. But it's really annoying when someone does it to you, I'll tell ya that!' Jed said, as graciously as possible.

'I think that's the point, Mr Simpfenator!' said Paloma playfully.

The afternoon classes seemed to fly by; Megs was on cloud nine. Only Miss Sheather still called him Edward now – his 'new' name was on everybody's lips. The non-Football Kids couldn't really get their heads around what it meant or why the Football Kids were calling him that, but Megs didn't care. No more Edward for him.

When the bell rang, Megs hung around talking with his new friends for a few minutes, then headed for home. But just near the gates, he saw the old cleaner, and stopped.

'Hi ya!' he chirped.

'Hi. You look happy, no? You had good day?' the old man asked.

'Yep. It was a good day.'

'You play vootball today? I no see you at recess, but I see you at lunch.'

'What do you mean, you saw me at lunch? We didn't see each other at all.'

'Ahhhh, you no see me, but I see you. I see you play

vootball. And I see you last Friday. You is happy when you play vootball, no?' he asked.

'You were watching us?' Megs felt quite pleased.

'Never know who's watching, Mr Megs,' the cleaner said, with the telltale shine in his eyes. 'You can play, yes, but must be careful not overdo it. Good to have confidence, but not good to always dribble when you can pass. Okay at school to do *szerecsen dio,* but not so okay in real match. Understood?'

'*Sa-ra-chan doh...* what's that? Sorry, I don't understand.'

A little smile crept across the cleaner's face – well more a grin than a smile, but enough to expose one or two crooked teeth. He used his broom to poke into some rubbish he'd swept into a pile, and knocked a Coke can free. He kicked it slowly towards Megs, who was still stationary and definitely still bamboozled. Then, with sleight of foot, the cleaner deftly flicked the can through Megs's legs, and elegantly spun around behind him to collect it again. For that instant, the man seemed young again.

'*Szerecsen dio,* Mr Megs,' the old man said, his eyes sparkling. 'You say "megs", but in Hungary we say *sa-ra-chan doh.* A good trick, but not good idea to do all the time – especially in games for points. It too risky to lose ball.'

Megs was impressed. The old cleaner didn't look like much, but he seemed to know his stuff, and he'd been watching. And *he* knew a nutmeg when he saw one!

'That's what Mr Mac always says. He's my old coach back in England. "Just don't do it too much," he'd say. He's right, but it's also too much fun sometimes – that's what I used to tell him!' Megs laughed at the memory.

'I know, I know,' smiled the old man, as his face wrinkled even more. 'Anyway, it good that you playing. No need to sitting when you can be playing.'

Megs noticed the old man was starting to shuffle and was getting ready to leave, when he remembered something.

'I don't know your name. We've been talking all this time, and I don't even know your name!'

'I'm Otti. Otti Seebar. I'm pleased to meet you, Mr Nutmegs.' The old man reached out and shook Megs's hand, bowing slightly as he did so.

Megs laughed, and replied in a fake, overly pompous English manner, 'Well, I am very pleased to meet you too, Mr Otti. Shall I see you tomorrow at this fine establishment?'

'Yes, I see you tomorrow, sir,' concluded the old cleaner, as he turned and hobbled away.

Yep, Megs couldn't help but like that old man.

Before Megs knew it, he was sitting in front of the computer again, impatient to turn it on and see what his mates had to say.

Ping, ping, ping, ping, ping, ping, ping!!

Seven messages. Brilliant!

Message one was from Woody.

> Hi Megs,
>
> Your mum told my mum why you haven't been in touch. Taking a day off is pretty full on, man! Well played. I didn't think you had it in ya. Do you remember when a few of us didn't turn up that time, but you were too scared? I just reckoned you were some weirdo that liked school, so things can't be too great over there. Still, a bit full on for your mum to not let us speak. She can be fullon.com sometimes!
>
> Nothing's any different here – except you ain't here!
>
> Woody

Message two was from Stevie R. Man, that guy was stranger on email than in real life!

> Hi ya Eggs.
>
> I know you hate me calling you that, dude, but I dig it, so respect. The world is wak boring, man, and school is the wak-est. Especially now that the Wanderers are done for the year. It's a downer, man, and I miss it already! How u doin w football? Any movement?
>
> U took a day to just go 'walk-a-bout'? You crazy dude – rock on and respect!
>
> Got a new phone. Just that the olds don't know about it yet. They're clueless I'm tellin ya!

So when r ya comin back to this hood, dude? Oz is only good for Home and Away, man!

Stevie R

Message three was from Jacko.

No need to get worked up about me not knowing about geography! I've never had to worry about time zones before u know. Fair question, I thought!

So you didn't take the day off with us that day, but you do it by yourself over there. That's twisted, man, but I guess it must be pretty tough for you over there. U going to do it again?

Weather still pants over here. Glad u haven't sent any photos yet – I'd just be jealous. School is just ticking over, and it's weird without football. Bit of a low now after the buzz of the championship. Glad you're playing a bit, but come on man, what's this about playing with some Aussie girls? Your mum told Woody's mum.

Message four was from an address he didn't recognise.

Dear Megs,

By the time you read this, you'll be back in the email world.

Now go and do some homework! :)

Dad.

Can you believe that guy? Megs thought to himself with a chuckle. *Sometimes he's a bigger kid than me!*

Megs quickly wrote back, purposely being even briefer than his father.

Dad, NO! Megs. :)

Message five was from Paloma and was titled 'Test'.

Hi Megs – just testing. Hope I remembered the address. Email back if okay.

Message six was from Matteo and was called 'Italian Megs'.

Hi Megs. In Italy they say 'toonell' for a nutmeg. They're trying to say tunnel in English and I think it makes a lot more sense than nutmeg. Don't know why they try to say it in English – maybe they think it's cooler. Dad reckons it's 'petit pont' in French, which he reckons means little bridge. Makes sense too. Whatever it's called, it's a cool trick. And being called Megs sure is WAY better than being called Nuts!

C u later, M

Megs was especially pleased to get the emails from his new friends. It was totally unexpected, and it made him feel sort of warm inside.

The seventh one was the biggest surprise of all. It was from Val, and even though Megs knew who she was (she was in his class), they'd basically never spoken. She had short dark hair and a doll-like face and usually went round with a book or folder under her arm. She was shorter than Megs, and quite skinny. She hung around with Paloma a lot, but Megs had no idea she liked football – she certainly didn't play at lunchtimes. She must've got his address from Paloma. Her email was titled 'GET THIS' and was full of weird football facts and statistics.

Megs,

I know you like soccer, so GET THIS!

- During the Euro 2004 tournament, the English Association ordered 24 bottles of styling mousse for their players.

- Manchester City goalie Bert Trautmann played the last 15 minutes of the 1956 FA Cup Final with a broken neck.

- In a really cold winter in 1963, Blackpool tried to use a flamethrower to thaw out a frozen pitch.

- Most goals in a single match by one player – 16 by Stephan Stanis for Lens in France in 1942. And DID U KNOW that the most goals scored by one player in an international match is 13, by AUSTRALIA's Archie Thompson! It's a world record. They won 31–0 against American Samoa – which is also a world record. Thompson plays for Melbourne Victory.

- Bill 'Fatty' Foulke weighed 157 kg at one stage in his 13 year soccer career!!

- The oldest professional was Stanley Matthews who played for 32 years. He played his last game for

England when he was 40, and stopped playing professionally when he was 50! My grandparents are 50 something!

- The youngest person to play in the English Premier League is Aaron Lennon. He was 16 years and 129 days when he first played for Tottenham in 2003.

- The shortest player was Jackie Bestall of Grimsby in the 1930s. He was about 1 metre 57. Paloma is taller than that! The tallest is Peter Crouch of Liverpool who is 6 foot 7 which is just over 2 metres.

- The highest ground is in Peru. It's 4633 metres above sea level, and Australia's tallest mountain is only 2229 metres!

- In Scotland, Dundee and Dundee United stadiums are just 89 footsteps apart.

- And there's one ground that is in two countries. Chester's pitch is in Wales, but part of the stadium is in England.

Did u know those things?

Val

Val's email was the most fun of all the ones he got. He didn't have much time (his mum had already called him to dinner), so he decided to write straight back to her and reply to the others later.

Hi Val,

How do you know all that stuff and how did you know I like football? Do you watch our games, or did

Paloma tell you? Those facts are cool. Do you reckon they're all right?

Here's a question for u – why do people in Australia and America call football soccer?

C u at school.

Megs

Things were much easier for Megs now that he had friends. He was feeling part of the Football Kids friendship group, the school work was still pretty easy, and he was turning into 'the main man' on the school football pitch. Life in Australia was picking up, and his old confidence was well and truly back.

And it was not just with the Football Kids that he was starting to enjoy himself, but with Otti, the old cleaner, too. Otti always seemed to have some football advice or words of wisdom, and always seemed in a good mood. Even without the football chat, Megs just felt good to be around the old guy.

And that's why what happened next was such a disappointment.

In fact, looking back on it later, Megs decided that he must have been relishing the group fun so much, that it all went to his head.

Just before the regular lunchtime game was about to start one day, someone mentioned the old cleaner and his knowledge of football. Next thing Megs knew, some of the kids were trying to imitate his accent, and screw up their faces to see if they could get the same amount of wrinkles (no-one could). Everyone was laughing, so Megs joined in. He began limping around, pushing an imaginary bucket and making fun of Otti's voice. His new friends were howling with laughter, so Megs kept going.

Then, quite suddenly, the Football Kids went quiet, but Megs continued, thinking he was still in the spotlight. When he realised that no one was paying attention to him any more, he looked up to see only stricken expressions on his new friends' faces. Their uneasy stares seemed to be going over Megs's shoulder, and when he turned, his heart sank.

The old cleaner was right there, watching the group.

Megs instantly felt worse than when his mum told him off for not going to school that day. He hadn't even meant to ridicule the old guy – it was just that everyone else was doing it. It was just for a laugh.

He looked at the old man's drooping shoulders and felt suddenly sick with shame. He stumbled to Otti's side. 'Otti... I'm sorry. I didn't... it was just a joke... it was... I'm...' Megs couldn't find any words.

The old man's head dropped and he looked away. Then, without looking at Megs, he said sadly, 'I thought you is different, Megs. We talk, and I thought you different. I in this country fifty years and you here five minutes, but you make fun of me. I friend to you and I thought you friend to me.'

With that, he turned and plodded back to the school buildings.

The other kids did not look at Megs. The lunchtime game got underway, but Megs's heart wasn't in it. He kept turning to see if Otti was watching, but he was nowhere to be seen. Megs felt terrible, and it was his own fault.

Eleven | Making a Difference

H i lads

It's me again from the other side of the world. Everything's going pretty well now. Well, OK. I've made some friends and play football with them at lunchtime. They're not bad … reckon some of them could play for our Wanderers for sure. I found out that the old cleaner is called Otti, and he knows heaps about the game. He's cool and weird. He's from Budapest in Hungary (it's in Europe, Jacko) but been here for 50 years or something. I think he might've been good, but he stopped playing once he got to Oz. 50 years not playing! Tried to google him and his favourite club, but not much luck. Seems to know his stuff.

Megs didn't tell his friends what an idiot he'd been in front of Otti the other day, and how they hadn't spoken since. It was too hard to explain, and it only made Megs look stupid. And feel stupid. So he continued:

I look at all the football sites, but can't find current editions of SHOOT and haven't seen any games. Apparently they're all on Pay TV, but my friend here lives up the street and she has it. I'll go and watch some games there I hope, but they're on at stupid times b/c of the time difference. Yes – she's a she – but she'd wipe the floor with you on the pitch, Jacko! She'd be OK for the Wanderers up front, I'm not kidding.

It's pretty much off-season over here now, and the main league doesn't start for a bit. It's called the A-League and apparently it's not bad. Sydney plays in blue – don't know if I can handle that. So the only place I play is at school. I'm megsing for fun, but it sucks not playing for points. There used to be a school team, but there won't be this year because no teachers want to coach. Imagine that back home! The Principal reckons there can only be a team if there's a coach – and he knows no one wants to coach, so he doesn't have to worry about a team. Not a football fan. So the guys have basically given up. Don't know what to do.

They do call it soccer here, but sometimes I hear it called 'wog ball'. Wogs are not Pakistanis and Indians like at home, they are everyone else but. Not people from England though – we're Poms. But there are so many people from all over the place here, I can't keep up with where they're all from. Everyone seems to speak heaps of languages as well as English – pretty cool really.

Good on Edge for winning Player of the Year. Fair enough, too. Especially for his first season with the Wanderers. Pretty annoying bloke, but he can play. I'm pretty happy with second – but annoyed I couldn't be there to eat my ice-cream-cake trophy! Sure you guys would've looked after it for me.

Gotta go. Mum's on my case about homework – you know what she's like.

See ya.

Megs.

In a few days, Megs got a reply from Woody, but nothing from the other lads. The replies were getting slower and slower, but he guessed everyone was busy. There was also one from Val, and he read that first.

Megs,

A good question about soccer. I'd never thought of it before. But I still got the answer of course. Get THIS.

What you call football was officially called 'association football' ages ago. So most people just called it football. But rugby was called 'rugby football', or sometimes 'rugger'. Then one day a guy answered a question about which football he played by saying 'soccer' which he took from the word asSOCiation and added an –er. It kind of took off a bit, and in places where football can mean other things (like American Football or AFL Football in Australia), they kept calling it soccer.

And while I'm at it – England didn't invent soccer, they just invented the current set of rules and the first proper association. That was in 1863 when it branched off from rugby football. I discovered that a similar game has been played in China for AGES – some articles say 1000s of years ago. Most people think that China is where the game was really invented.

Keep the Qs comin!

Val

Wow! Val sure did know her stuff, Megs couldn't deny that. Well, either she just knew everything, or she was really good at finding things out. Either way, he liked getting emails from her, even though they barely even spoke to each other at school. He'd reply later, because he wanted to see what Woody was up to first.

Hi Megs,

I agree. Football's great at school, but scoring goals into a net and playing for 3 points is way cooler. Why don't the teachers do it? Maybe your dad'll coach? Surely someone'll do it. You can't not play because of a pox reason like that.

The old bloke sounds cool. Does he ever join in? Maybe not – he must be older than our parents by far. Did you check the spelling for the google search? Who knows what Budapest people spell like.

Glad u r making friends and that things are going OK. Nothing is different here.

Woody

Megs wrote straight back.

Hey Woody,

I'll ask Dad to coach, but he's busy with his new job, so I don't like my chances. It's a good idea though – I'll ask the other kids about their dads. You're right, I've gotta think of someone. Without competition, I'll go a bit stale I reckon.

Spelling! Hadn't thought of that … I'll check with Otti.

Checking with Otti would be tough seeing as they weren't speaking, but Megs didn't want to think about that.

Went to Paloma's the other night (the Football Kid up the street) and watched the Spanish League. Real Madrid and Valencia. Very different to Premier League, much slower, but great to watch. Paloma's family are cool – and MAD Real fans. Weird to think of Beckham playing there. They spoke Spanish most of the night (especially when they were yelling at the ref), but it was pretty entertaining. Paloma told me what they were saying, and we laughed a lot. We never stopped eating, either. I think they have a constant dinner at her house – all sorts of snacky stuff I've never had before.

Better go. Write soon. Hi to everyone,

Megs

After Megs had pressed 'Send', an idea came to him. *Maybe Paloma's dad will coach? He seems to love the game, and his daughter would be in the team...*

'I've been thinking...' Megs started, as he and Paloma were walking to school the next day.

'Don't hurt yourself!' Paloma interrupted.

'Ha, ha.' Megs continued, 'Anyway, I was thinking about when you said that the school can't have a team unless we have a coach. No teachers will do it, and you reckon that Mr Jackson is pretty happy about that. Well, what if it's not a teacher that coaches? Do you reckon we'd be allowed to have a team then?' he asked.

'Hadn't thought of that,' Paloma replied.

''Cos I reckon we'd be pretty good, and playing just at school isn't the same. The school should have a team,' Megs said.

'But we've already been told we can't. Before you came. We'll just have to wait and then join local teams or something. Though it would be cool playing in a school team, wouldn't it...?'

Paloma seemed to be talking more to herself than to Megs but he replied anyway. 'Sure would! Was hard enough meeting you lot! I don't want to go through all that again.'

Then he thought it was time to ask another question.

'I asked my dad if he'd coach, but he can't 'cos of work. But I was thinking, do you reckon your dad'd do it? He knows a bit about the game, doesn't he?'

'Yeah, he knows heaps. But you heard him the other night – he doesn't speak good English, and I don't want to translate all the time. He'd be at work, too, I reckon. Nah, we'll have to think of someone else.'

'Maybe we should bring it up at the game today,' Megs suggested, as they entered the school gates.

Megs and Paloma were two of the first down to the football ground at lunchtime. Paloma was now just as excited as Megs about the possibility of a proper school team. Surely they could find a coach.

When everyone was there, Paloma said, 'Umm, you know how we were told we can't have a proper school team this year because there's no one to coach? Well, Megs thought of something last night. Just say there's a coach who's *not* a teacher? Surely then Mr Jackson would *have* to say yes to a school team – and then we could play real games!'

There was a murmur among the Football Kids, before Jed spoke out. 'But they already told us we couldn't play as a school team.'

'They told us we couldn't play because there's no coach – they'll have no argument if we get a coach,'

Paloma reasoned.

'What difference does it make?' Jed continued, 'We don't *have* a coach, remember?'

'Well, what about our parents?' Megs asked. 'Do anyone's parents know anything about the game? My dad can't because of work, and Paloma's dad doesn't speak enough English. Anyone else?'

The Football Kids talked among themselves for a bit, but the general feeling was that no one's parents could do it. Either work would get in the way, or they knew nothing about the game. Or in the case of poor Adam: 'Are you kidding? I don't even tell my dad I play. He thinks I play rugby every lunchtime!'

It looked like Megs's plan was over before it had begun.

'Well, everyone ask anyway. It's the only way we can have a team, so you might as well ask,' he said, stubbornly not willing to give up just yet.

'Fair enough,' Jed said. 'But enough standing around... let's play!'

That night, Megs tried to break his juggling record again. But he just couldn't concentrate, and didn't even beat 120. He was getting a bit bored with just kicking his ball against the wall, or occasionally having a kick with Paloma. And while the lunchtime games weren't boring, there was just something missing. For the first time in weeks, Megs found himself once again thinking of home, and missing football. So he decided to cut his losses, and leave his ball alone for the night.

Back inside, there was nothing on telly, so he went to the computer instead. He actually intended to get some homework out of the way, but couldn't help checking out the web for a bit first. Not much had changed since he'd checked his favourite sites immediately after school, but it was still better than homework.

Then he remembered Woody's email: *maybe it's the spelling*. Megs hadn't asked the old cleaner about the spelling of his name, because he hadn't spoken to him in days. Otti used to go out of his way to speak to Megs, but in the last few days when they'd seen each other, he had just turned and walked the other way. Megs missed speaking to the old man, and he only had himself to blame. He knew he had to apologise, but hadn't managed to work up the nerve yet. Apologising when you know you are wrong and when you know you have really upset someone is not easy. But it had to be done somehow…

So Megs followed Woody's suggestion, and decided to get back onto Google to try a few different options. He had to wait a couple of minutes for his mum to finish up what she was doing. Ever since she had started the computer course, she could hardly be peeled away from the keyboard.

This time he started with 'Hungarian Football', then

tried to find the club Otti had talked about. Most of the sites came up in a weird language, but some were in English. And Otti was right – Hungary did beat England 6–3 at Wembley. Megs hadn't really wanted to believe it when the old man had told him, but there it was right in front of him! It seemed that around that time, Hungary was beating everyone, and most articles seemed to mention that Puskas guy. In fact, Hungary had lost *just once* in forty-eight matches between 1950 and 1956, and that was an upset in the 1954 World Cup Final. Then, it seemed there was some sort of war, and the team fell apart. There were lots of web articles explaining how so many people escaped or at least tried to escape from Hungary at that time. *I wonder if Otti was one of them?* Megs thought. It looked as though Hungarian football was never the same afterwards, anyway. Something pretty bad must've happened, and Megs remembered Otti saying, 'Hungary was run by bad men for a while, but that doesn't mean that everyone is bad' – or something like that.

Megs managed to find something about Kispest, and saw that the club had become Kispest Honved after two clubs joined together. It used to be an army-based team, and had some very strong players – including the man whose name seemed to keep popping up – Ferenc Puskas.

Megs got back on the email to tell Woody what he'd discovered.

Hi Woody.

Found some stuff about Hungarian football and about what Otti says is his old club. Didn't understand a lot of it, but that guy Puskas comes up all the time. Have u heard of him? He played at that club (Kispest-Honved), but didn't go back to Hungary after 1956. Some of his stats are cool. His dad played for the same club, and he was playing seniors at 16 (he left school at 12! That's roughly next year for us!). He made 349 appearances for them over 10 years and scored 358 goals. He played for Hungary when he was 18 and in 84 international appearances he scored 83 goals. How cool is that!

Have you seen any photos? He's really short and looks pretty fat, and he was all left foot apparently. Didn't stop him though. Hungary won Olympic Gold in 1952 and were runners-up in the 1954 World Cup when everyone thought they'd win. Can u believe they beat England 6-3 AT WEMBLEY and then 7-1 in Hungary!!!!!

Kispest Honved were playing a European tie in Spain when some sort of fighting started in Hungary, and even though it was basically an army team, some of the players didn't go home because of all the problems – including Puskas. They just stayed in Spain. Don't exactly know what happened in Hungary, but it must've been pretty bad. Puskas didn't play for 18 months. He was unfit and 30 odd, but then started playing for Real Madrid. He helped them win 6 championships and 3 European Cups and retired at 39. In 372 matches for them, he scored

324 goals. Incredible! They say that's what started Real Madrid being a top club today. He ended up playing in another World Cup, too, but this time for Spain. I didn't think you could play for more than one country.

I wonder if Otti knows him???

See ya,

Megs

Woody must have been on the internet before school in England, because he wrote straight back.

Ping!

Hiya Megs,

I've been having a look too. Who would've thought they were that good! Puskas and Di Stefano come up all the time, huh. Couldn't find out much about the actual club either, BUT ...

Puskas coached in Australia. Did you know that? Not sure for how long, but the team was called South Melbourne. I saw some photos, and he looked really fat! Couldn't imagine he was such a legend. Have a look at www.smfc.com.au and see what I mean. I think there are quite a few photos about it around the web as well.

Woody

Megs couldn't believe such a legend was involved with Australian soccer, so he continued the search – and discovered that his English pal was right. Puskas had been in Australia for three seasons coaching South Melbourne in the late '80s and early '90s, and they had won the championship, too. The league was called the 'National Soccer League' and there were big crowds in the photos. Maybe, just maybe, football *was* actually popular in this country.

'Megs – bedtime please!' his mum called from the kitchen. Time really does fly when you're having fun.

'Come on, Mum... a few more minutes?' Megs pleaded. It never worked, but he always tried anyway.

'No. Off to bed. You have school tomorrow,' she replied.

Megs managed to sneak in one more email before bed. He thought he'd test Val about Australian 'soccer'.

Hi Val,

Here's another q for u. How long has 'soccer' been in Australia, and how long has the national team been called the 'Socceroos'?

Good luck. :)

Megs

The next day on the way to school with Paloma, Megs explained all that he'd found out about the old cleaner's favourite club, about Hungarian football and about Puskas. Paloma wasn't that surprised.

'The way my family goes on about Puskas, you'd think he was some sort of god. I didn't actually know he was Hungarian, but I had a feeling he wasn't Spanish because of his name,' she said.

'He played for Spain, though,' Megs said.

'Really? Huh. Dad never told me that. You said he played for Hungary.'

'I know – he played for both. Weird, huh. Wish we could see players like that play. It'd be cool to see if they were as good as Gerrard or Beckham,' Megs said dreamily.

'Or Raul, Cannavaro, Ronaldo or even Zidane from a year or so ago,' added Paloma. 'They're all Real stars – I wonder if that old team could beat the current one. Or even beat the Socceroos with Kewell, Neill, Bresciano, Schwarzer or Viduka. Surely those old guys weren't as good as the current players!'

'Guess we'll never know,' said Megs. 'But our parents will always tell us they were!' he concluded with a smile.

Throughout the morning, Megs couldn't get images of Puskas in Australia out of his head. Short and fat and with all those admirers crowding around.

But there was one photo that stuck in his mind the most vividly. He wasn't sure why it did because there wasn't a crowd, and there wasn't a football in sight. It was just the fat man hugging someone else in a restaurant or somewhere like that. But the image kept floating into his head, so he asked Ms Sheather if he could stay in the classroom at recess and go on the internet.

''Course you can,' she said. 'I'm impressed. Just don't look up anything inappropriate, okay?'

Megs quickly found the photo again, and his heart skipped a beat. The guy Puskas was hugging – was it...? He looked even closer, and was convinced.

But he needed someone to ask. Or someone to tell. Someone to confirm what he'd seen. So he went outside, found Paloma, and dragged her away from Val and the group of people that were always around her.

He then turned back after a couple of steps and said, 'Val, you might want to see this too.'

'What's going on?' Paloma asked as Megs hustled them away.

'You have to see this,' he told them urgently, speaking in double time. 'You know all that stuff I was saying about Puskas, and Hungary? You sent me lots of stuff, Val, and so did my friend Woody back home. It all started after Otti talked to me. Something about what he was saying made me keep thinking about it. Or maybe it was the way he said it, I don't know. But anyway... you'll never guess what I just found... take a look at this,' he finished excitedly as they reached the classroom.

The screen saver was up, so Megs flicked the mouse to show the photo.

There was a small silence as the girls stared at the screen. Finally Paloma spoke, sounding confused.

'That's Puskas, but so what? He doesn't look like a soccer player, that's for sure, but what's the point?'

'Who's he hugging?' Megs asked.

Paloma bent forward to look, then jolted back.

'No way!' she exclaimed.

'See what I mean! It has to be, doesn't it?' Megs asked.

Val had a closer look, then gasped. 'Whoa! Really! How about that. There might be more wrinkles now, but it's obviously him. Look at the teeth, and the moustache...'

The caption read *Old Timers Catch Up Hungarian Style*.

They all stared at the photo of Otti, their school cleaner, as he had been twenty-five years ago, being greeted with affection by one of football's greatest players.

And this is the man who was so kind to me right from the start, thought Megs, *who I made fun of just days ago.* He wished for the hundredth time that he had stopped to think before trying to win some popularity points by slipping into the role of class clown.

Until now, he hadn't read the rest of the article because he had been fixated on the picture. So with Paloma and Val looking over his shoulder, he scrolled down.

Hungarian soccer superstar Ferenc Puskas took time out from coaching South Melbourne to catch up with an old team-mate yesterday. Puskas spent a decade playing for Kispest Honved in Hungary before moving to Real Madrid in 1958. He shared some old stories with Atti Czibar, an ex team-mate who also left Hungary after the 1956 revolution, and ended up in Australia. While Puskas continued on to superstardom in Madrid, his old Honved team-mate never played again. 'Atti was a very good young player,' the South coach said. 'He was just a kid in the mid-'50s, but he could play. It's a shame he didn't get to play for Hungary more, and a bigger shame he never played again after he left. But it's great to talk about the old days.'

The story went on to discuss South Melbourne, but the three kids had read enough.

'Atti with an A!' Megs exclaimed. 'I've been spelling it wrong! And I didn't even come close with his surname. I *thought* it was S-E-E-B-A-R!' He turned thoughtfully to the girls. 'I thought he knew what he was talking about!'

'I wonder why he never played again? How can you just not play for fifty years?' asked a puzzled Paloma.

At that moment, the bell rang to signal the end of recess, interrupting their discussion, but not diminishing their excitement.

'Let's not say anything to anyone just yet,' Megs said. 'Remember he's still not talking to us.'

'Okay. But I just can't believe it.' Paloma sounded

sad. 'An international soccer player pushing a bucket around at our school!'

'I'll see what else I can find out tonight,' Val promised, as they headed for their classroom.

After dinner, Megs managed to scrape through some homework, writing a couple of paragraphs about the latest stage of his 'Around Australia Car Rally'. He discovered Melbourne became a settlement in only 1835 (and officially known as Melbourne in 1837), and began to realise how much older the towns in England are. His dad had told him he thought that Melbourne used to be Australia's capital until the new capital – Canberra – was created in the bushland between Sydney and Melbourne because no-one could decide which should be the ongoing capital. Melbourne and surrounding towns boomed when people found gold in the 1850s, and Megs tried to imagine people coming from all over the world, pushing all they owned in little carts into the bushland to find their fortune. People would often walk for days and days under the hot sun, and Megs wondered if any of them took a ball with them to have some fun. Then, for a break, he checked his email.

Ping! It was Val.

Hi guys,

I've managed to find a lot of stuff on Puskas (did you know that Real Madrid won the first FIVE European cups?) but not much more on Atti. His name comes up on a list of Hungarian players, but everything was written in Hungarian, so I couldn't be sure when he played or how often. And I don't think the club has very good records. I'll keep looking around though – the Internet never lets ME down!

Oh, and just while I was at it – GET THIS!

- Numbers were first worn on the back of shirts in 1928.
- Goalkeepers were allowed to use their hands all over the field until 1912.
- In 1949 a Hungarian player moved to an Italian club for a doughnut-making machine. And in 2001 Zidane cost Real Madrid $117,200,000! That's a lot of doughnut-making machines!
- In the 1930 World Cup Finals, the referees wore a suit jacket and tie!
- And India refused to play in the 1950 World Cup because FIFA told them they had to wear boots instead of bare feet.

Sorry, I couldn't help myself. Will let u know about Socceroo question later, Megs.

Val

Of course, the best thing to do to find out about Atti was to talk to Atti, but Megs was still in his bad books and it was going to take some courage. He was 99 per cent sure the old cleaner was that former international player – and he couldn't believe that Paloma hadn't even thought of a possibility that Megs just couldn't shake out of his mind.

Something he had become very excited about since seeing that newspaper article...

Something staring them right in the face...

Something that would solve all of his problems...

Maybe Atti would coach us! Maybe with him we could *have a real team!*

Megs was genuinely sorry about how he'd treated the old cleaner, and he was pretty sure everyone else was too. No one had made fun of him again since that day but nor had any of them spoken to Atti or attempted to apologise.

Atti had been avoiding Megs, and Megs couldn't just walk up to him and say, 'Hi Atti. Listen, sorry about imitating you. Now... can you do us a favour by coaching the school team?'

But there had to be a way – a way to show he was sorry, and hopefully a way to make an old player want to take up football again.

The next day was Saturday morning, and Megs slept in. But when he finally got up, he immediately staggered, still rubbing sleep from his eyes, to check his email. He hoped the lads had contacted him, but they hadn't. He was in touch with them less and less, and he'd only been in Australia for about a month.

The only message was from Val, and was called *The Socceroos. What time does that girl get up in the morning!* Megs thought. People were so bright and active in the morning in this country – such craziness would take some getting used to.

You can't beat me, Mr Megs!

Football has been played in Australia since the convicts arrived on the First Fleet – 200 years or so, I guess. Then lots of other people from all over Europe came and the game got stronger and stronger. There was some sort of battle between clubs in the 1960s and lots of dodgy transfers, so the Association was thrown out of FIFA. A new association was formed in 1963, and we've been in FIFA ever since.

In the old days the team was just called the 'Australian National Team', but they were called the Socceroos from 1969 onwards. Seems a journalist just started calling them that when they were on an Asian tour, and it stuck. Cool, huh – the Association – Federation – or whatever they're called had nothing to do with it.

And while I'm at it, GET THIS. Our first World Cup effort began in 1967, but we didn't get very far. We made the 1974 World Cup and got a point against Chile, and then the 2006 World Cup, of course, where we did really well and made the second round. The biggest loss was against England in 1951. 17-0!!! But we beat England 3-1 in 2003 – I'm sure you remember that. :)

Heaps of Aussies have played overseas, starting with Joe Marston in the 1950s. He played for Preston North End for 5 years. (Did you know they won the first two English Championships in 1888 and 1889?) Others, like Krncevic, Yankos, Farina and Davidson, started going in the '80s, but the biggest star was Craig Johnston – you should know him. He played for Liverpool and won all sorts of championships. Did you know he was Australian? Now over 100 Aussies play overseas.

You'll have to do better than that to stump me!

C u at school.

Val

Wow. Craig Johnston was Australian! Liverpool was the *team of the '80s, and there was an* Australian *playing for them? How about that!*

The news about the 17–0 defeat against England made him smile. He decided to keep that pearl of information tucked away in case he needed it at a later date. That Val was a machine!

Val,

Don't u ever sleep? U have to get outside more often!

We have to talk about Atti – I need some more information about him. I need a good way to make up with him.

C u l8r

Megs

He left the computer to organise some breakfast. His parents were sitting reading the paper in the sunshine that streamed through the kitchen window.

Mrs Morrison looked up in fake surprise. 'Well, it walks! Good sleep, lazybones?'

'Not bad,' Megs mumbled.

'Thought we'd get out and have another look around today,' Mr Morrison suggested enthusiastically. 'What d'you reckon? We could go to the zoo, or the museum, or up Sydney Tower.' It looked like that Aussie early-morning energy was rubbing off on these two as well. Couldn't they just relax?

'Don't know. I guess,' Megs replied indifferently. He just wanted to resolve the Atti dilemma – and he kept thinking Val and Paloma might be able to help.

Megs's mum became brisk. 'Well, you have to get some homework done this morning, then we'll see later.' She had been turning into the homework police as well as the bedtime police of late.

'Should've stayed in bed...' Megs grumbled to himself.

If his parents heard him, they chose to ignore it and went back to the trivia questions in the paper. They obviously didn't have a clue about Australia yet, because they got a grand total of zero correct – and thought it was funny.

Bet they wouldn't be laughing if I came home with zero on a test! Megs thought irritably, as he spooned some more cereal into his mouth.

With his breakfast finished and after some more prompting from his mum, Megs settled down to get some homework done. He hadn't done much all week and Miss Sheather was starting to get 'disappointed' in him (her words). So it was time to pay his dues. Once he got into it, it wasn't so bad, and a couple of hours passed quickly. By now his 'Holiday' had taken him on to the Great Ocean Road which he learnt was built by 3000 soldiers returning from World War 1. The road hugs the cliff with the ocean looming below, and people even died during its construction. The road goes all the way down to the famous Twelve Apostles – a bunch of rock stacks, proudly sticking up from the pounding surf. Megs had only managed to count seven stacks in the photos he'd seen, but maybe some of them had fallen down since they were named. So far, Miss Sheather hadn't made him service the old 4WD he'd 'bought', so happily, he still had plenty of money for the rest of his trip. His concentration was finally broken by the sound of a knock on the back door.

Megs heard his mum's voice from down the hall. 'Hi Paloma, honey. How are you?'

'Good, thanks. How are you?' Paloma replied in her best politeness-to-parents voice.

'Good, good. Do you want to see Megs?'

'Is he here?'

'Well, he's just been doing some homework, so I'm sure he'll be happy to see you. The study is just down the hall.'

'Hi ya,' Megs said as he came out of the study to meet his friend. 'Did you come for a kick or to do my homework for me?'

'Possibly later for the kick… and no way, to the homework! I came over because my dad just told me there's some sort of soccer special on cable TV about the background to Liverpool. They're going to show the training grounds and the city, talk to the players and all that. It's on in ten minutes, so Dad said you could come over for lunch and watch it.' Paloma was very excited for Megs, and with good reason – he was ecstatic.

'Cool! Mum – can I go? I haven't seen the Reds in ages? Can I?' he begged.

'I wouldn't mind seeing that, either,' said Mr Morrison in the background. 'Do you think your dad'd mind, Paloma?'

'Nope – they hoped you might come too. They always cook too much paella on Saturdays, so it'd be good to eat it all for once! What about you, Mrs Morrison?' By now Paloma was bouncing around happily.

'Well, I don't really want to stay here while these two have all the fun. And it *is* the Reds.' Megs's mum made a quick decision. 'Come on – we'd better hurry!'

Megs was surprised at his mum's new enthusiasm for the Reds. She'd never been to Anfield to watch games, and only sometimes went to see Megs play; maybe she was feeling a bit homesick or something. But as they all left 20 Valletta Avenue and hurried towards Paloma's house, Megs couldn't help smiling to himself. This was way better than going to museums or the zoo!

Twelve | What To Do?

The Morrisons had a great time at Paloma's. Megs was starting to get a taste for olives, and even his meat-and-three-veg dad had enjoyed quite a few as well. He certainly had a lot of Mr Mendez's red wine, that's for sure, and wouldn't shut up about how good it was. Mrs Morrison picked at her paella nervously at first, but soon got into the spirit of things as well. Megs was shocked when Paloma was offered a taste of Mr Mendez's wine as if it was no big deal, and he was very conscious of his mum's glare at that same moment. She was clearly saying, 'Don't even think about it!' without even opening her mouth. Talented, really.

It was weird to see Liverpool the city and Liverpool the club on television from the other side of the planet. It made Megs feel very distant from what he was used to, but he still didn't feel sad. It was impossible to feel sad with all the friendly noise and activity at Paloma's house.

He did miss the football though, and the afternoon strengthened his determination to find a coach and build a team. When he saw how competitive the Liverpool players were at training, and how seriously they took matches, he realised again how much their sport meant to them. And it meant that much to him, too. If he was going to make it to the top one day, he needed to play for points in some serious matches before he lost his edge.

On their walk home Megs's thoughts were interrupted by his dad.

'The Reds were looking good, huh? That Gerrard is even the best at training. Such a hard worker – the game really is in his blood.'

'I know. But he *is* playing for the best club in the world, so why wouldn't he want to put in?' Megs replied.

'It was nice to see Liverpool again,' reflected Mrs Morrison as she unlocked their front door. 'I didn't realise how much I'd blocked it out since coming here. Strange though, it didn't really feel like home as much as I thought it would.'

'I know what you mean.' Mr Morrison smiled. 'But – following the Spanish theme, and in the spirit of in-for-a-cent-in-for-a-dollar – I'm going for a little Spanish siesta. I can tell we're going to like living up the street from that family – even if I could only understand about half of what Pablo said. Thank goodness Paloma was able to help out!'

'Don't worry, Dad, he probably understood even less of us!' Megs laughed.

'It was a lovely afternoon, but then I went and invited them all around for a meal next week –' Mrs Morrison realised aloud. 'How am I supposed to top this afternoon's feast? I should've kept my mouth shut!'

'Your lamb roast never fails, honey,' Mr Morrison said as he gave his wife a squeeze. 'Right, then... I'm off until I'm up again. Got to love a lazy Saturday!'

Megs felt good seeing his mum and dad so happy, and it really had been a good afternoon. But there was no time for Megs to take a nap – he had a plan to get back onside with Atti, and there was no time to waste.

'Hello, South Melbourne Soccer Club,' came the high-pitched voice on the other end of the phone.

'Hello, my name is Edward and I'm looking for Mr Puskas, please.' Megs thought he did a pretty good impersonation of an adult voice, and was pleased he'd thought of saying he was Edward and not Megs. Much more grown-up.

'Who did you want, sorry?'

'Mr Puskas,' 'Edward' replied, keeping it brief.

'Puskas. Is he a player here? Sorry, I haven't heard of him. I haven't been here long.'

'He was your coach a few years ago. Helped you to a championship... legend of world football...' 'Edward' was starting to sound more and more like Megs again as he got a bit agitated.

'Just give me a sec,' the lady said.

Doesn't know Puskas and works at a football club?
Megs thought as he paced the room, waiting.

'Hi... you there?' the lady asked.

'Yes.'

'I'm told he left here years ago and went back
overseas. If you want some information for a school
assignment, maybe you could use the internet. Thanks
for your call.'

'Yes, bu...' Megs started, but the dial tone on the
other end of the line told him the lady had already hung
up. *Some help she was... school assignment indeed... and
how did she know I was a kid?* he wondered.

This was a blow, but The Plan hadn't died yet.

After some searching, Megs discovered some more
recent information about the famous Puskas. Pretty sad
news, actually, but still relevant to the plan. Puskas *had*
left Australia years ago, and gone back to his native
Hungary after years and years away. *'His greatest
personal achievement was returning to his homeland at
sixty-six years of age,'* one website said. His homecoming
wasn't all streamers and marching bands, though. The
great man had been struck down by an illness called
Alzheimer's disease that meant he required full-time
medical support in a Budapest hospital. Even sadder was
the fact that he'd had to sell some of his prizes and
memorabilia to cover his expensive medical costs –
trophies, photos, uniforms and a golden boot awarded

to him for his world record goals tally. All went up for sale. *That doesn't seem fair.* Megs felt sad for the old champion.

He couldn't find anything more on the whereabouts of Puskas, or anything else on Atti either, and he was getting tired.

Time to include someone else in Plan A, because the thing was – there was no Plan B.

Hi Val,

I've got a good q 4 u. A challenge.

After we saw that picture of Atti w Puskas, it got me thinking that maybe Puskas might be able to fire Atti up about football again, and help me apologise to him. I mean, the two are friends, right, and the article did say Puskas thought it was a shame Atti didn't play again. If football's in your blood, it's in your blood, so maybe an old team-mate from Hungary might help Atti accept that. Cos I reckon he misses the game, and has done for the 50 years he's been here.

Thing is, I found out Puskas is back in Hungary and is pretty sick with Alzheimer's disease. Whatever that is, it doesn't sound good.

So your challenge is to find him so I can call or email him. Reckon you're up for it?

Keep it quiet for now.

C U Monday.

Megs.

Megs was the first to admit that Plan A was seriously flimsy, but it was a plan all the same, and it felt good to be doing something instead of sitting around feeling sorry for himself that he hadn't made up with Atti yet.

He was pretty confident that Val, the Information Machine, would be able to find Puskas, so Megs took the time before dinner to get a letter ready for when she did.

Good afternoon (or morning), Mr Puskas,

My name is Edward Morrison, but everyone calls me Megs because I like to nutmeg people all the time on the football field. I think in Hungary you call a nutmeg 'sarachan doh' (sorry if the spelling is wrong), but I think you of all people will know what I mean.

I am sorry to hear that you are sick, and was very surprised to find out about it after I had read all about your amazing career. I also recently saw a photo of you with a friend of mine during your time in Australia, and that's why I'm writing.

I moved to Australia about a month ago from England, and it was hard to make friends at school. But there is an old cleaner at my school who was always nice to me, and he really helped. He knows about the game as well – I could tell as soon as we starting speaking. I found out that you used to play with him at Honved and even a couple of times for Hungary, I think. His name is Atti Czibar and he has lived here since 1956. He never played again after leaving Hungary, and I think that makes him sad.

I was stupid recently, and he caught me making fun of him behind his back. I didn't mean it, but I can see why he's angry with me. I want to make up to him, but don't exactly know how. I thought you might be able to help.

Also, my new friends and I need a coach so that we can make a real team instead of just playing at lunchtime, and I wish that he would do it. I think he'd really like it, but I haven't asked yet because we aren't speaking at the moment.

I hope you can understand this letter. I did lots of drafts to get it just right.

I hope you are OK, and I am happy for you that you've been able to go back to Budapest. I also heard that you have had to sell some of your football stuff, and that doesn't seem right. I have sent you a 2005/2006 Liverpool Yearbook signed by Steven Gerrard. Maybe you could sell that instead.

Yours in football,
Megs.

When he'd finally completed the draft, Megs sat back in his chair. He was pretty proud of himself. He was particularly happy with the 'yours in football' bit – he'd seen it once before in a letter to *Shoot* magazine and thought it was very cool. Like football was the connecting thing that every football-lover understood. And it was that football connection that Megs hoped would help him make up with Atti – and at the same time get an international player as coach of the Football Kids.

Surprisingly, Megs didn't even think for long about including his precious yearbook. Hearing that Puskas was having to sell things that he'd earned had messed Megs around a bit. After all, Megs had done nothing to earn that yearbook other than just be a fan, but Puskas had been so good that millions of people around the world were fans of his. The fans owed *him* something, surely.

Ping! An email had arrived.

It was called 'Not good' and was from Val.

Hi Megs,

That's so sad about Puskas. Alzheimer's disease is pretty bad. It gradually makes people lose their memory and become confused and there isn't a cure. It's pretty full on, and I've read he has an advanced form of it, as well as some other illnesses.

I haven't tracked him down yet, but I'll let you know later.

Not sure how this all helps with Atti.

Val

Megs wasn't exactly sure how all this was going to help with Atti either, but he was willing to give it a go, and hope that Atti's football blood ran deep. But Puskas's illness certainly sounded bad, and Megs wondered how long he'd had it for. And he wondered how much of his career he remembered these days. How many of those incredible moments he'd worked so hard

139

to create – gone, just like the trophies he was selling. It sucked that so many people seemed to remember how good Puskas was, but that he himself might not remember it any more.

Megs had never really thought about old players when they stopped playing, kind of assuming they'd always just be players. They didn't age in posters. And strangely, it made him just a little bit more confident about becoming a star himself one day. After all, the players were all human just like him. They weren't invincible superheroes after all. 'They all put their undies on one leg at a time like we do,' his old coach Mr Mac used to say, and Megs was starting to see what he meant.

Thirteen | Something a Bit Different

There were just a few Football Kids playing at lunchtime a couple of days later, because some of the others were on an excursion. So Jed the Simpfenator, Megs, Paloma, Max and Matteo had set up a goal and were doing some crossing and finishing. Mostly, they were trying to score with their heads (except for Paloma, who wasn't interested in it), but sometimes also by trying to imitate the spectacular volleys they had seen on TV. They sometimes rotated the goalkeeper position, but Max spent most of the time in there, and was getting pretty good at it too. His size sure helped.

'Watch this – watch this!' the Simpfenator called out excitedly, like a six-year-old trying to impress his parents with a dive into a pool. 'Matteo, see if you can put it up in the air around here.' He gestured with his hand at head height.

Matteo tried to cross the ball to Jed, who was standing with his back to the goals, and although he got pretty good height from his position away to the right, he only succeeded in skewing the ball way off target.

'No, no, try again,' Jed said. 'Knock it back out to Matteo,' he instructed Paloma as the ball bounced towards her. She obliged – though rather grudgingly.

Matteo tried again, but once again bent the ball to the left of the Simpfenator. It seemed that all Matteo's efforts to lift the ball off the ground were decreasing his usual accuracy.

Remembering what Mr Mac had told him once, Megs called out to Matteo, 'Leaning back is good to get some height, but you have to point your toes more and keep your ankle really strong. Otherwise the ball will go all over the place.'

Matteo prepared for another go as the Simpfenator started to get frustrated. 'Come on, Matteo,' he said edgily. 'It's not that hard.'

Matteo didn't even appear to hear Jed's complaints, and somehow maintained his calm. Megs wondered how he did it. Matteo approached the ball, keeping his ankle really strong as Megs had suggested, and tried to strike under the ball as he kicked it. This time, the ball travelled much closer to the Simpfenator, but not close enough for him to try whatever it was he was so keen to do. Jed raised his arms in frustration, but Paloma didn't see the gesture because she had her eyes on the ball. She was a bit further out from the goal than the Simpfenator, and the ball was coming straight to her.

Quickly, she adjusted her position, and, maintaining focus, she stared intently at the path of the ball all the way until it connected with her swinging right foot. Her body position and balance were just like on TV, and her head was low over the ball.

BANG!

In one smooth motion and without trying to kick the ball too hard, she connected beautifully, and the ball flew towards Max in goal. What a strike!

Max's reflexes took over in the goals, and he automatically stuck his big hands up above his head as the ball sped towards him. WHACK!

The ball smacked into his wrists and hands with such force, that his arms were pushed back, and his whole body staggered for a couple of wobbly steps. But the ball sprang straight up, and stayed out of the goal. It was still in play though, and Megs reacted quickly, running towards its flight, leaping as high as he could to meet it, and easily nodding it back towards the goal. With Max off balance and Megs only about a metre away from the goal line, it was an easy way to finish off Paloma's spectacular shot.

'Wow! What a strike, Paloma!' Matteo yelled.

'Yeah – you sure got hold of that. Just like on telly!' agreed Max as he rubbed his stinging hands.

'Huh! That felt great – I reckon that's the only time in my life I'll do that!' Paloma smiled.

'Reckon even Raul would've been proud of that!' Megs continued enthusiastically. 'And what a save, too, Max. You're getting pretty hard to beat in there.'

'Next time, try to put it where I ask you, Matteo,' was the Simpfenator's grumpy contribution to Paloma's wonder-strike and Max's reflex save.

'Relax, Jed,' Megs said. 'What are you trying to show us, anyway?'

'Nothing,' was the curt reply.

'Nothing huh? Come on, man, this is s'posed to be fun. Relax a bit, and show us,' encouraged Megs.

'Well, I was watching *Victory* last night – not the A-League team, but the movie. Do you know it? It's an old war movie with Sylvester Stallone in it, but heaps of soccer players too. Old guys I hadn't heard of but who were all professionals, so my dad says. I saw the credits at the end though, and there were guys like Ardilles from Argentina and Bobby Moore from England that I'd heard of. The main one was Pele, though. Have you seen it?'

No one had, but Megs was intrigued. 'Bobby Moore is a legend in England. He captained us to the 1966 World Cup win. And Ardilles played for Tottenham for a while, I think. What's it called again?'

'*Victory*. Or *Escape to Victory*. I can't remember. It's old and pretty lame, but there's some cool stuff too. *Anyway*, Pele did this cool thing in it that I want to try.'

Megs was a bit stunned. How is it that he was being told about an old football movie he'd never heard of, in a school playground in Australia... he'd have to ask the lads back home about it or see if the local DVD store had it in stock...

'So what'd he do?' Paloma asked.

'Well, he kind of kicked it over his head towards the goal behind him when he was in the air. He, like, sort of jumped up as the ball was coming over, and looked a bit like a high jumper – you know how they lean back as they clear the bar? Well, he looked a bit like that. Then, when he was kind of flat in the air with his head towards the goal and his legs the other way, he twisted his body and kind of swung his legs above his body to kick the ball towards the goal. It was cool as!'

'But wouldn't you land on your head?' Paloma asked.

'I don't think so. Well, he didn't, anyway. As he kicked the ball above his head, he twisted around and ended up falling onto his side.'

'Yeah, I've seen players do that as well. It's brilliant!' Megs added. 'It's called an "overhead kick", or sometimes a "bicycle kick" – I guess because your legs need to go up and over as if you're on bike pedals.'

'I've heard it called a "scissors kick", I think,' added Matteo. 'I saw it in the Serie A the other week, and also in the movie *Goal*. They're all over *YouTube* as well.

'Sounds more like an upside-down karate kick to me,' suggested Paloma, sounding a bit worried.

'Whatever – I want to try it,' Jed said, getting even more excited.

'Well, how about I just throw the ball up from here to make it easier?' Matteo suggested, moving closer so that he was standing only a metre away from Jed.

'Good idea,' Jed said as he turned his back to the goal

and prepared to be a movie-star legend. Max got ready in goal, while Megs and Paloma stood by for the action.

'Righto!' Jed called to Matteo.

Matteo threw the ball just where Jed had pointed, then stood back to enjoy the show with the others.

Jed sprang up just as he'd described, but totally mistimed his jump, and missed the ball completely. He flopped onto the ground with a thump... flat on his back, and looking more like a fallen star than a superstar. The others couldn't help laughing.

'Good one, Simpfenator!' Paloma joked. 'I can see why that'd be in a movie. What a cool trick!'

Megs continued the fun. 'Yeah – you should write a coaching book!'

'Shuddup. Give me another go.' Jed's face set in a determined scowl.

Matteo threw the ball up again, and this time Jed jumped a little earlier than before. As he swung his leg around, he misconnected and the ball smacked onto his knee and flew straight into the air. He was much better at the twist-as-you-fall part this time though, and fell onto his side quite comfortably.

'Again!' he demanded, bouncing back onto his feet.

On the third attempt, he managed to get his foot to the ball, but it just went straight back to Matteo on the right instead of over his head to the goals. But Megs could see what he was doing, and wanted in on the action.

'Not bad, Jed. My turn.'

Megs kept his eye on the ball as he rose like a high jumper and prepared to boot the ball back to Max's goal. But, mid-jump, he became concerned about how he would land, and instinctively twisted his body to protect himself. At that point, the whole idea of kicking the ball became entirely irrelevant. He managed to land chest-down and softened the fall with his hands, but a split second later, the ball dropped down and clocked him on the back of the head.

It was his turn to face the laughter.

'You reckon *I* looked stupid!' Jed howled.

'Ha ha!' Max joined in. 'Stick to nutmegs, man – you looked like a fish being pulled out of the water!'

Paloma was enjoying these two making fools of themselves. 'You two sure aren't Pele, that much is clear!'

'Want another go?' Matteo asked.

Megs and Jed were both quick to reply. 'Yes!' they yelled.

So the rest of lunchtime was spent trying to perfect this new skill, or – more accurately – get the skill right just once. But they were having fun diving around all over the place. Matteo and Max had a go as well, but Paloma decided that such a stupid-looking thing could be grouped with headers as something she wouldn't do unless she absolutely had to.

By the time the bell went, none of the boys had got a shot on target, but Jed *had* once succeeded in getting the ball over his head and in the general direction of the goal. It was enough to show them that the move had some value, and they swore that one day they'd get it right.

After the bell went, they plodded back to the classrooms, covered in dirt and grass stains, still laughing at how stupid each of them had looked, and ribbing Paloma for not even trying.

As they were about to walk into their room, Megs stopped Paloma and pulled her to one side where no one could hear them.

'I want to talk to you about Atti, and what we should do. Can you, Val and I meet tomorrow before school?'

'What do you mean – what we should do? What is there to do?' Paloma seemed genuinely puzzled.

'What are you on about? We've talked about this … I reckon we should see if he'll coach us, but I can't ask while he's not talking to us, can I! I dunno what to do, and I reckon if we all talk about it, we might think of something – it's now or never, and I don't want never.'

'Okay,' Paloma agreed, just as Miss Sheather appeared at the classroom door, beckoning them in. 'I'll come to your place early, and we'll meet Val here. I'll send you both an email or text or something later, with a time.'

'Thanks.' Megs gave her a grateful punch on the arm. At least they were doing something about sorting their muddle.

Fourteen | Plan B

'**B**ut how's it going to work? I mean, what difference is that going to make to the guy when he hasn't played for fifty years?'

There was still a little while to go before school started, and the three friends were conferring on their usual seat overlooking the football ground. But the discussion was not filling Megs with confidence. He went on, 'And how do we give it to him when he's not speaking with me? Or any of us, for that matter!' He couldn't help seeing the difficulties in the girls' idea.

But Paloma and Val were convinced. To them it seemed simple. Val explained it again: 'Look, we go on the Internet, maybe go to the State Library, and collect whatever we find on Atti and the time when soccer was so big in Hungary. We put it all together in a scrapbook or something, then give it to him as a gift – a sort of sorry gift, a sort of trophy or tribute.'

Paloma added, 'And maybe we could also put in some general soccer quotes or something. Anything to help get him fired up. Maybe we could do something in Hungarian as well.'

'Something in Hungarian? Are you kidding?' Megs couldn't believe his ears. 'Since when do you know Hungarian? You Aussies can barely speak English!'

'The net, Megs.' Val was visibly trying to keep her temper. 'I'm not saying we have to do the whole thing in Hungarian, but maybe just some words that we can copy from a translation site.'

'But how does that say sorry and persuade him to coach the team? And how do we give it to him anyway?' Megs was trying to get the picture.

Paloma and Val were excited now, and were determined to get their message through to Megs.

'There had to be a good reason for him to stop playing, right?' explained Paloma. 'But no one who plays at the level he did can just stop thinking about the game. You said he's always talking to you about it, right?'

'Was,' Megs muttered.

'Well, maybe this will help him get fired up about the game again!' Paloma reasoned. 'I know he stopped playing when he came here, after the war in Hungary, but you can't turn off something you love! Look at you when you came here – you couldn't just leave it behind.'

'Yeah, but why would we make any difference after all these years? Surely heaps of people have tried to get him involved again.'

'Look, Megs, it's the best idea we've got, and you don't have anything else. Why'd you get us together this morning if you didn't want to try something?' Paloma was beginning to sound fed up.

Megs gave in. 'Okay, okay, settle down. I guess it won't hurt to give it a go. But how do we get the information, and how do we give it to him?'

Val took over. 'Well, I like a challenge, as you know, and the internet hasn't beaten me yet. I got the address for your letter to that guy Puskas a week ago, didn't I? Took some emails and chat rooms, but I got there. This shouldn't even be as hard as that.'

Val's right, Megs thought. *If anyone can do this she can.* The girls' enthusiasm was starting to soften his grumpiness, but his thoughts were interrupted by a question from Paloma.

'What letter?'

'Well, I've already sent something off to Puskas,' Megs replied. 'Dunno why, really, but I guess I was hoping he'd be able to help somehow.'

'Really? Good stuff. I wonder if it'll get through?' There was real warmth in Paloma's voice.

'Hope so. But who knows if he'll even read it, if it does. But look, back to Atti – how do we give him the scrapbook?'

'Well, I reckon we put it together first, then leave it somewhere for him to find. That's probably better than being there when he first looks at it in case he doesn't like it... or hopefully gets emotional about it!' Val grinned. She was really into this. 'I'm happy to get onto Google right away. You know I love this sort of stuff, but

I might need a hand later too.'

'No problems. Looks like we're all sorted.' Paloma nodded decisively.

'Yeah, cool,' Megs finally agreed as the bell went to signal the start of another day. 'Can't hurt to give it a go. Over to you, Val.'

Pal and Megs,

I'm getting some good stuff, and even some photos. Not heaps, though, and there's a bit in Hungarian which I think I'll include anyway. I don't know what it says, but hopefully Atti'll like it! Looks like a song. Seems he had quite a future. Maybe he could've become a real pro.

Anyway, it'd be good to get some quotes and stuff about the game just in general, like we talked about the other day. Can you guys do that? I might need some help with some of this stuff... not that I've been beaten or anything... just that I've got a lot of homework this week.

C u 2moro.

Val

Megs replied:

Ha!

You finally ran out of juice! But yep, 'course we'll try

to find some other stuff on different sites.

Megs

Megs didn't mess about, and got straight into action. Inspirational or motivational quotes were easy to find, and even though most of them weren't directly related to football (and were written by people he didn't know), he found that lots of people have said lots of great stuff to really charge the batteries. *Maybe Dad is always so upbeat because he spends a part of every day reading these things,* Megs thought.

It was hard not to be upbeat after reading so many positive things, and it gave him new hope that they were on the right track with Atti... and therefore on the right track towards getting a real team.

He copied some of the best quotes into an email to Val:

Hey Val, what about something like this on the first page? It's a classic football quote by the old Liverpool boss, Bill Shankly.

Some people think football is a matter of life and death. I don't like that attitude. I can assure them it is much more serious than that.

Or this one is pretty good...

The difference between the impossible and the possible lies in a man's determination.
- Tommy Lasorda

This next one would be good too. It's by a Pope!

Concern yourself not with what you tried and failed

in, but with what it is still possible for you to do.
– Pope John XXIII

I think this is the guy who's on the telly a lot. Makes sense, eh?

You see, in life, lots of people know what to do, but few people actually do what they know. Knowing is not enough! You must take action.
– Anthony Robbins

This one could go near the end somewhere.

It's not whether you get knocked down; it's whether you get back up.
– Vince Lombardi

And this one would be good to finish it all off, I reckon, because it can relate directly to coaching.

The best and fastest way to learn a sport is to watch and imitate a champion.
– Jean-Claude Killy

Megs then checked his in-box for other messages. It'd been a couple of weeks since he'd got anything from England, and he wondered if that was just the way it was going to be from now on. To be honest, though, he hadn't been missing his old friends as much as he'd expected. So much was going on at school. There were odd moments when scenes from his old life popped into his head, and it gave him a strange, twisted feeling in his belly. Sometimes Megs felt like a grain of sand in the desert, being blown to and fro, as he forged a new life on the other side of the planet... but, as his dad often said, 'Well, this is where you are, so it's your choice what you do about it.'

And, to be fair, thought Megs, he hadn't written to his mates in the last few weeks either, so it wasn't *all* their fault. He was starting to run out of things to say that would be of interest to them back home. How would he explain what had happened with an old Hungarian footballer who hadn't played in fifty years and pushed a bucket and mop around his school? How could he explain that he was doing his best to get the old man to be their coach so they could have a proper team? Would his old friends care that he'd offended the old man, and now they weren't speaking, so things were pretty tough? And would they be interested that his new friends (both girls!) were helping him out? Or that his new friends were really good value and that he was starting to enjoy Pennendale – maybe even more than his old school in Liverpool? He felt guilty even thinking about it, let alone trying to tell his old friends.

The State Library wasn't as stale and musty as Megs thought it would be. He was pleasantly surprised by how open, light and – well – *cool* it looked. The person at the front desk wasn't old, fat or deaf, but looked about twenty-five, and had rings in his eyebrow as well as long, dark hair and a tattoo on his wrist.

'Hey!' he greeted the three friends. 'It's Val and some little book-loving buddies! How are ya, then, *Valeria?*'

He sounded just like Paloma's Spanish dad when he said her name, and Val blushed.

'Hi, Jez. I'm good.'

'School assignment?'

'Kind of. We need to do some research on an old sportsman,' Val replied.

'Cool. Well, you know your way around my place!' The librarian spread his arms in a friendly, comical gesture. 'But I'm here if you need me, little dudes!'

'You know that guy?' Paloma asked as they walked into the library proper.

'Well, it's not just on the internet you can find things out, y'know,' Val said. 'There are things called books, and there are plenty of them in this place.'

'You spend a lot of time here, then?' Megs asked quietly as they made their way across the enormous reading room.

'Sometimes.'

'Sometimes? That guy knows you pretty well for "sometimes"!' Megs persisted.

'Well, so what? I like it here. You like running around chasing after a stupid little ball – and I like coming here.'

Val spoke so indignantly that Paloma and Megs shot a glance of surprise at each other, and Megs decided to keep his mouth shut from now on. After all, Val was doing all this for them. She wasn't even going to be in the football team, and she wasn't Number One in Atti's bad books. Just because libraries weren't *his* thing...

156

A couple of days later, they met early at school again to see what they had come up with. Well, Val had done most of it, but they were in it together, and Megs was getting very excited about the possibilities after seeing how much information that library had.

'You can put your phone away now – we're here,' Megs stated with an edge of frustration in his voice. Paloma had been texting during the whole walk to school, and Megs didn't think she really got the significance of what they were trying to do. Or maybe she didn't believe that what he wanted was possible.

'Hang on...' she replied as she finished off another message. 'Right. What were you saying?'

'Nothing. Just about the library the other day. Forget it.'

They walked through the school gates and saw Val waiting for them, holding a grey folder.

'Hi, guys. Excited?'

'Megs isn't. Got out on the wrong side of the bed this morning, I reckon!' Paloma imitated his sour face.

'Well, what am I s'posed to be like when you're texting the whole way to school!' Megs replied gruffly.

'See what I mean?' Paloma asked Val with a laugh.

'Come on, let's just go through this stuff...' Val grinned at both of them.

'I'm not grumpy, you know,' Megs said as they walked to their usual seat. 'I guess I'm just nervous about all this. Excited too.'

Paloma looked at him sideways. 'Clown!' she commented, almost affectionately.

'He'll be jumping out of his shoes when he sees what I've done,' said Val.

They sat down and, with Val in the middle, went through the folder. Even knowing how clever Val was, Megs was amazed. She had done a superb job putting everything together. She had put one of the quotes Megs had found on every page, as well as some that Paloma had uncovered. Under each quote there were copies of old newspaper articles in Hungarian and English, and even a couple of match reports and photos from the 1950s.

'Wow, Val – this is incredible!' Paloma pointed to a grainy black-and-white photo showing a bony player on the move – the ball in close control. 'Is that Atti in this shot?' They all stared at the big, balloon-like shorts and what looked like workboots on the player's feet. It looked like there was a big crowd, too.

'Well, the caption says his name, so I'm guessing it's him.'

'He's just a kid! There's no wrinkles or anything. And look at him go!' Paloma's voice squeaked with enthusiasm.

'And look at the smile on his face... you can even see his crooked teeth,' Val added, with a contented smile of her own. She turned the page, and there was a black-and-white team shot. 'See if you can find him in here…'

Paloma and Megs looked intently, but it was Paloma who spoke first. 'Here. It's him. It's got to be him, doesn't it?' Her finger was touching the skinniest, youngest-looking player in the shot. His black hair was slicked back, and there was no spindly moustache, but the smile was there, and the eyes looked as bright as they were today.

'Yeah, I think it's him too,' Val agreed. 'I don't know for sure, but it's a team from the correct era and a team he played in, so I had to guess he was in it. And it sure looks like him.'

Every page turned was another story in itself, and with the quotes accompanying the photos or articles, and decorative borders on every page, Megs was constantly getting little shivers down his spine but, unlike the girls, he was unusually quiet.

'What d'ya think, Megs? You haven't said anything,' Paloma finally asked, as Val turned the last page and closed the folder.

Megs was staring down at the folder, trying to work out why he felt subdued. Finally he replied, 'He's smiling in every photo. There's no doubt it's him, and he's smiling in every photo. It's funny, but it makes me a bit sad.'

'C'mon, Megs! Are you kidding? A guy's smiling and you think it's sad? You really *did* get out on the wrong side of the bed this morning!' Paloma was laughing, while Val seemed mystified.

'No, you don't get it.' Megs wanted them to understand. 'When I came to Australia, I didn't think I was going to play football again, and it made me sad to think about it. I used to sit there and watch you Football Kids running around playing and that made me even sadder because I wasn't playing too. But since I started playing, everything here is different. Good different! And I think Atti is just like that – but he hasn't played for fifty years. I see him smiling in every photo and it makes me sad because it was so long ago.' Megs shuffled his feet and prayed they would understand. It was the first time he'd actually told anyone how hard it was to come to Australia, and he felt a bit weird.

'That's pretty full on, Megs,' Paloma said at last. 'No wonder you've been so keen on all this.'

'Yeah, I guess. He helped me out, then I made him feel bad. I just reckon it'd be good to repay the favour, y' know? This is absolutely brilliant, Val. Brilliant. No wonder you get top marks in everything. Let me go and leave it in his room right now. If this doesn't fire him up, and show him that we're sorry, then nothing will.' With that, Megs got up and walked directly to the little room where Atti kept his mop, his bucket and whatever else he had in his 'office' for cleaning the school.

Fifteen | What Now?

'What's going on with you, Megs?'

Mr Morrison went into the family room where Megs was hunched on the sofa staring at a *Simpsons* repeat, and turned off the TV. Megs looked up, startled. His dad sat down beside him on the sofa and looked at him searchingly. 'You've been moping around here like someone's died. No one's died, so what's the story? You've hardly said a word in days; you've been skimming through your homework; you push your food around your plate, and I've not even seen you have a kick for a week. So now I *know* something's wrong! Do you miss everyone back home? Is that the trouble?'

'I'm fine.' Megs refused to meet his father's eyes.

'No you're not. Get your ball – we're going outside.'

'No thanks, Dad.'

'It wasn't a question, young man. Get your ball and let's go.'

Megs had to admit that his dad was no slouch with the ball, but he wasn't in the mood for a kick with him at the moment. It'd been four days now, and Atti hadn't said a thing to anyone about the scrapbook. They were sure he'd got it because Val had seen him carrying it home beneath his arm... so why hadn't he come to see them? What else did he expect them to do?

Megs's dad was persistent, so Megs finally followed him outside.

'Wake up, will you?' called Mr Morrison. 'It's no fun by myself! Here, take this on your chest!' he said as he clipped a pass over to his son.

As the ball drifted towards Megs, he couldn't help himself. He positioned himself in the flight of the ball, then leaned back slightly to cushion the impact. The ball struck him on the chest, then bounced straight up into the air to about head height. Slowly then it dropped down towards the ground, where Megs's foot was waiting to control it.

'Good one!' Mr Morrison called out. 'You've always been good at that.'

Megs rolled the ball back with his right foot, then quickly flicked his toes up from underneath it. The ball popped up into the air high enough for Megs to take a big swing through it, and send it flying back towards his dad.

Mr Morrison tried to control the approaching ball by cushioning it on his head – but only succeeded in losing balance as the ball hit him, and falling flat on his backside.

'Quality, Dad!' Megs laughed. 'You'll be playing for the Reds any time now!'

'Yeah, thanks, son. They need the odd clown in there to keep things real, huh. Let's see how many we can get on our heads together…'

After half-an-hour of playing with his dad Megs had to admit he felt better for it.

'So, are you going to tell me what's wrong?' Mr Morrison finally said as he belted another ball towards the house wall.

'Watch the windows, you two!' Mrs Morrison shouted out of the kitchen window. 'I've got two kids to look after, I swear I do!' The players rolled their eyes at each other.

Megs controlled the bouncing ball as it came back from the wall, then smacked it back again. 'It's nothing,' he told his dad.

'It, huh? Can't be nothing if it's an IT.'

'Well, it's a long story.'

Mr Morrison stopped the ball, and sat his backside down on it. 'Well, if I go inside now, I'll just have to help your mother get dinner, so the longer you can make the story last the better.'

Megs laughed and pulled up a patch of grass next to his dad. 'Fair enough, but don't sit on my ball – you'll put it out of shape.'

At last it all came out. Over the next fifteen minutes, Megs explained everything that had happened with Atti, and how disappointed he was that the old cleaner hadn't said anything about the scrapbook. How they'd put a lot of time into it, so Atti could've at least thanked them. He even told his dad about the letter he'd sent to Puskas. His dad listened intently the whole way through, only responding with the occasional 'hmm' and 'aah'.

'So that's basically it,' Megs concluded. It felt great to get it all off his chest.

Mr Morrison looked at his son in silence for a minute and when he spoke, Megs thought he could hear pride in his dad's voice.

'You sure have gone to some effort,' Mr Morrison said, 'and this obviously means a lot to you. I didn't know you missed competitive matches so much, but it doesn't surprise me.'

Megs nodded. 'It's not that I don't enjoy having a kick with the kids at school –'

His dad's hand landed reassuringly on the back of Megs's neck. 'I know that. Your mother and I are really proud of how you've made friends here and given it a real go.' Then his father turned towards him, speaking more slowly. 'But I have to say, Megs, I'm not surprised the cleaner hasn't come to see you and thank you for the scrapbook. *You* know you feel bad about what you did, but does *he* really know that? If he hasn't played football for fifty years, he must be a pretty stubborn, proud guy.'

Megs was surprised at his dad's comments and wanted him to stop and backtrack for a minute, but it seemed *he* was now on a roll.

'Tell me,' said Mr Morrison, 'what happens if you're in possession, and the defender tackles you, but you think it's a foul? What do you do? Does someone like Gerrard lie there complaining?'

'No, you get up and chase back and try to get the ball back again. That's an easy one, Dad. Complaining to the ref isn't going to help.'

'Exactly. And is it hard work to chase back trying to get the ball?'

'Yeah...' Megs replied, wondering where this was heading. 'Of course it's hard work – no one likes it!' Pretty stupid, question, really.

'But what's it like when you get the ball back?' Mr Morrison persisted.

'Brilliant,' Megs said.

'Well, your situation with Atti is kind of like that. The scrapbook was a great idea, but a bit of a cop-out –'

Megs began to bristle with indignation, but his dad went on. 'It was a substitute for the real hard work, Megs. It was not the really *courageous* thing to do.' He looked intently at his son. 'See what I'm saying?'

'Not really.' Megs was reluctant to grasp his dad's point.

'You made a mistake with the old guy, so you have to be courageous enough to chase back after the ball. You have to go to him and apologise to him face-to-face.'

Megs's heart sank. He'd been afraid that was what his father meant.

'It won't be easy, Megs,' Mr Morrison spoke gently, 'but it has to be done if you want to get Atti's friendship back.'

'I do!' Megs stood up abruptly and belted the ball into the wall of the house. Immediately his mother's face reappeared at the kitchen window.

'Ease up, Ronaldinho!' she called.

Mr Morrison put one foot on the ball and waited until Megs was facing him again. 'And also,' he said, 'it's your only hope of getting him to coach your team, isn't it?'

'Yeah, you're right, I guess.'

As they walked back inside, Megs made up his mind. *It's what Gerrard would do,* he thought.

The next day at school, Megs didn't play with the Football Kids. Instead, he went to his old spot in the corner where he used to sit alone a couple of months ago when he was the new kid. He sat down and waited, watching the action in the playground. But he didn't have to wait long. A squeaking bucket and mop had come to a stop in front of him and he looked up to see Atti standing there. He could not quite make out the expression on the old man's weathered face.

'Hi, Atti,' Megs said shyly. Not exactly eloquent, but it was talking just the same, and he was underway.

'What you doing here? Thought you'd moved on to down there.' Atti gestured towards the Football Kids.

'Well, yeah, but I wanted to see you... just like before.'

'Why you want to see me?' Atti asked.

Megs got to his feet. 'Did you get the scrapbook?'

'Yes.' Atti looked away. 'You made a lot of work.'

'It was mostly Val.' Megs felt he had to explain. 'Paloma and I just helped her – she's great at that stuff.'

'Hmm.' Atti seemed to have no further comment. Megs fought back his disappointment. Dad had said it wouldn't be easy. Finally Atti looked into Megs's face and asked, 'What you want?'

Megs stood up straight and spoke as clearly as he knew how, making an effort to look into Atti's face rather than at his own toes. 'I want to say I'm sorry, Atti. I want to say sorry for making fun of you. You were the first one to help me out in this new place, and I shouldn't have done it. I didn't mean to be cruel, I was just joining in – you know, making friends.'

A faint twinkle appeared in Atti's dark eyes. 'Not good way to make friends.'

'I know. It was dumb.'

'I thought you different, Megs,' said Atti, ignoring him. 'You all alone here, then you start to play, and we talk vootball. I don't come down to watch vootball because I stop much years ago, but that day I decide come down to see you play, and instead I see you making fun of me. I not feel good.'

'Sorry,' Megs muttered again. Man, this wasn't easy at all!

'But thanks for the scrapbook.' Atti's voice softened. 'It bring back many memories I mean to forget. But I cannot forget, it seems. Lucky you not see me when I first look through the book – not good to see a wrinkled old man with funny accent crying!' Atti chuckled.

Seeing his crooked smile again, and knowing that the scrapbook had meant something to him after all, made Megs feel much better. He joined in Atti's laughter, as the old man began to rattle his bucket, signifying he was about to move on.

'Thank you for apologising, Mr Megs... now go and play. You not want to waste time here with me. Go and play.' Atti waved playfully towards the football game.

'Thanks, Atti!' Megs said, as he bounded off. Then, abruptly, he stopped and turned. It was now or never.

'Atti, wait! There's something else!'

The old champion paused, and Megs rushed on before his courage failed him. 'The Football Kids can't have a proper team without a coach. We want to play in proper matches.' He hesitated, then decided – *in for a cent, in for a dollar...*

'Will you be our coach, Atti?'

There. He'd done it. That wasn't so hard. Just like removing a bandaid – rip it straight off as quickly as possible and all of a sudden it's over.

Silence…

Then more silence…

So Megs began to ramble. 'You'd be great and we'd all love it if you coached us. The kids all more or less know you were a top player, and it'd be great to show Mr Jackson there's enough interest to make a team. It's cool playing at lunchtimes, but it's not the same. You know what I mean. I could join a team on the weekends when the season starts up for real next year, but it's been hard enough making friends with these guys, and they're the ones I want to play with – in a proper team, y'know? And I think we could be pretty good – we've got some good players. So will you do it, Atti? Will you coach us?'

When Megs finally dried up, he saw that Atti was staring straight into his face. But there was no twinkle in his eyes now. His piercing stare made his face crinkle almost as much as when he smiled, and Megs felt uncomfortable. Did this seriousness mean good news or bad? The seconds of waiting were killing him.

'So what d'ya think, Atti?' he prompted.

Atti shuffled his feet and fiddled with his mop handle – actions Megs had seen plenty of times before. He looked down at his bucket, then back up to meet Megs's expectant gaze. His voice was very low.

'No.'

And that was it. Megs was dumbfounded. Soon, the only sounds were the bucket grating on concrete and kids playing in the distance. He had screwed up bigtime. There was no coach and there would be no team. Slowly he walked across the playground to the Football Kids. Most of them had figured out why he was with Atti, and now he'd have to give them the news.

'How'd it go?' called Paloma as Megs reached the ground. The game had stopped and the kids crowded around, focusing eagerly on Megs's face.

'Well, we're speaking again, and he really liked the scrapbook. But he said no to coaching the team. Looks like it ain't gonna happen.' Megs's voice was hoarse with disappointment.

'Well, at least you're speaking again.' Good old Paloma – always trying to look on the bright side.

'Told ya,' was Jed's comment as he looked around the sombre faces. 'Come on, let's play!'

The game began again, but Megs drifted around the field with his mind elsewhere. He was pretty sure that Paloma was devastated, too – the usual energy was gone from her game – and some of the others, like Max, Matteo, Biscan and Abda, were obviously very disappointed. The sting had been taken out of their tails, and the game had lost its zing. *The game's less fun when your heart's not in it,* Megs thought. He remembered something Mr Mac used to say: 'Without heart, you're just a bunch of robots chasing a piece of old leather around a field. With heart, you might just merit the name of "footballers".' Just another saying from the guy who was now likely to be his first and his last real coach. Megs hadn't realised how important coaches were until he didn't have one.

The game continued at half-pace, until a shot from Biscan limped past the bag that made up the outside of the goal. The ball dribbled away, and Matteo jogged off to retrieve it and take the goal kick. Nothing was being done with any real zip.

Matteo placed the ball for the restart, but then, as he stepped back to begin his approach, a clear old voice rang out strongly from the side of the field: 'Spread out, give him option!' It stopped Matteo dead in his tracks. His eyes widened, then looked around in search of Megs and saw that a broad smile was spreading across his team-mate's face.

Soon everybody was smiling, giggling and whispering to each other. It was Atti, limping towards them, grinning from ear to ear, his wrinkles obvious even at ten metres. The old man was making only his second appearance at the Football Kids' field. The last time, everyone had been making fun of him; this time, it was as if he'd turned them all into zombies. But there was something different about him. Without his beaten-up bucket and mop he had become a person with a life of his own – just Atti, not 'Atti the cleaner'.

The old man made it to the edge of their pitch and stopped.

His back straightened, and his chest puffed out slightly.

'I hear you need coach, no?'

Megs was the first to react. 'You'll do it?'

'Why not, huh?' Atti's voice was strong and positive.

'You all love vootball, I love vootball, and now we show everyone why vootball should be loved, no? You need someone to take the team – if you want me, you have coach!'

'Want you! Are you kidding!' Paloma ran to hug her new coach – in fact, her first ever *real* coach. 'Thank you, thank you, thank you!'

Her gesture triggered pandemonium. The cheers were so loud that everyone else in the schoolground stopped and stared. Atti was so swamped by kids that he staggered on the spot every time a new one ran in to join the cheering mob.

Kids began hugging other kids, and the boys starting wrestling madly as energy surged through their bodies. They kept booting the ball high into the sky, and there were more 'high fives' being thrown around than in the American basketball team. Atti's smile was plastered across his face.

'Okay, okay,' he finally said above the din. 'Enough before you kill me! I old man, you know! You go play now. First I see Mr Jackson. Later we hold team meeting. Go on now – go play before I join and show how to *really* play vootball!'

The Football Kids didn't have to be told twice, and the game began again at twice its former speed. The ball wizzed about the pitch and the players moved almost as fast.

All, that is, except Megs.

As Atti headed towards the principal's office, Megs

left the match and jogged after him. 'Thanks, Atti,' he said. 'Why did you change your mind?'

Atti turned to face his young friend. 'When you leave me the scrapbook, I not thank you at first. It bring back too many memories that I try to forget. It make me sad – first because I missed those days in Hungary, but second because I missed vootball. I say no because I not want those memories to come back. My life here different.' He sighed and then his twinkling smile appeared.

'But, Mr Megs,' he continued, 'when I walk away from you after saying "no", I cannot get your little face out of my head. To see you first sit in corner without friends in new country, then later see you play vootball with such joy and make friends too. So I guess it your fault, Mr Megs, that after fifty years I involve myself with the game again. So I need to thank you – and not just for scrapbook.'

Megs didn't know what to say, so he just stood there silent. It was as if he had concrete in his shoes, and no tongue in his mouth, but his head way up in the clouds. Everything had worked out perfectly.

Atti turned to go, then remembered something. 'One more thing... someone who know a sick old friend of mine in Hungary write to me. Someone called Edward had write to him with the hope he could persuade me be coach. You wouldn't know anything about that, would you, Mr Megs?' His eyes twinkled as he waved an envelope in the air. 'You might want read this...' He handed Megs the envelope and walked away.

Megs glanced over at the delirious Football Kids and was dying to join in the fun, but he just *had* to know what the letter said. Quickly, he tore it open and began to read. When he was finished, he shoved it into his pocket and sprinted back to the game beaming.

Just a few months earlier when he'd won the championship with Wendesley Wanderers in his old home, he didn't think he'd ever feel so good again. But as he rejoined his friends, he realised just how wrong he'd been. For the first time he realised that it's not *just* winning football matches that can make you feel on top of the world.

Epilogue

Megs had read the letter so many times over the last few months he could recite it off by heart, but he still liked to feel the stiff envelope and to examine the neat black handwriting. He'd tucked it into his sportsbag before he left for school that morning, along with his boots and brand-new Pennendale Primary football strip. The bag had stayed under his desk all day in preparation for a fast getaway to the game that afternoon, and it wasn't the first time he'd taken a peek at the letter.

Dear Atti,

You not know me, but you do know a patient of mine who received a letter about you from a boy in Australia called Edward Morrison. My patient was Ferenc Puskas, and as you know he died recently. It a very sad time, but a few weeks ago I see his joy to receive Edward's letter, so I decide I write to you because I know Ferenc would have want me to.

Edward wrote because he needs coach for his school team,

and thought Ferenc might persuade you to do it. So for Ferenc and for Edward, I write to you – I hope not too late and you said no already. (Sorry for my not perfect English – it not my best language!)

Some of Ferenc's strongest remaining memories at the end were on football and on the people in football. When he hear that you still not work for the game in Australia, it made him sad. The boy who writes the letter loves football, and Ferenc knows you love football too. Even after no play for so long a person does not stop loving the game.

For the sake of your old team-mate, please think about what the boy Edward asks. Ferenc has been an inspiration to us here, and we want to share that spirit with others. Maybe you create some new, happy memories for yourself along the way.

Yours in Football,

Istvan Acs

Kutvolgyi Hospital, Budapest

As Megs slipped the letter back into his bag, a warm tingle danced down his spine. He stole another glance at his new strip, and couldn't help but smile. He found his thoughts easily drifting off throughout the day, and mostly it was about two things – their first game, and Woody.

It'd definitely be weird not to be playing in the Wanderers' yellow and black, and positively crazy to have to play in blue, but Megs couldn't ask the school to change their sporting colours just for him. The lads back in Liverpool couldn't get their heads around that, but Megs was smart enough to realise he shouldn't push his luck after Mr Jackson had finally said yes to them having a team. He'd said as much in his last email to Jacko, Woody, Stevie R and Dan last night, and Megs was rapt he was back in more regular contact with them. He'd sent a long email with some photos the day after Atti had said he'd coach, and told them all about the letter from Puskas. Surely they'd think *that* was pretty cool... and he was right.

To add to the excitement of the last few weeks, Megs had also received the great news that his friend Woody was coming out to Australia from England for a holiday. His dad was coming for work, and Woody had managed to persuade his family to let him go too. He was going to stay with Megs for *two whole weeks*, and Megs spent lots of time daydreaming about what to do with his best mate. He couldn't wait to show him around.

'All the players in today's soccer game please meet at the front gates to walk down to the ground. Atti will be waiting for you. Anyone who wants to go and watch the team in their first game will have to wait and go to the ground after school has finished. Mr Jackson and some of the teachers will be making their way down straight after school, and can escort those students. Good luck,

Pennendale Primary!!'

It was the classroom announcement that all the Football Kids had been waiting for. Every one of them in Miss Sheather's class sprang out of their chairs and bolted for the door. Megs grabbed his bag, and led the way.

'Easy, easy!' Miss Sheather called. 'Don't injure yourselves before you even get to the game! Good luck to you all – and have fun!'

As Megs made his way to the door, Lin spoke to him for the very first time. Ever since that first day when she hadn't been happy about Megs sitting next to her, she had avoided him. 'Good luck, Megs. I'll see you at the game.' Megs was surprised, and actually quite impressed. Even *she* had called him Megs.

'Thanks, Lin,' was all he could manage as he raced outside.

Atti was waiting at the gate with a big bag of balls. He was sporting a brand-new blue tracksuit jacket with the team's logo on the front and *Braithwaite Machine Tools* on the back. *Braithwaite's* was where Mr Morrison worked, but it was Vincent who had got the idea of sponsoring the team. He'd bought them the balls and the uniforms, and even negotiated with the local council to get use of the grounds. When Megs had thanked him after hearing the great news, Vincent had tousled Megs's hair and joked, 'Well, it'll be worth it to see a Liverpool fan like you wearing blue!' It was funny to think how Megs hadn't liked him when they'd first met.

During the short walk to the ground, everyone was joking, laughing, and bursting with excitement. They were on their way to their first game as *a real team* playing *for points* in their *first real season*. Atti led the way, with Megs, Paloma and Val walking proudly beside him. Val wasn't part of the squad, but had been allowed to leave school early with the team because she was going to report on the match. In fact, she was going to report on every game for the school's newsletter, and she was taking the responsibility with typical seriousness. Her notebook and pencil were tucked neatly into her bag, and she was already proudly wearing her team tracksuit top.

The boys used the home-team change-rooms first, and had to be quick so that the girls could have a go as well. Megs pulled his new shirt out of his bag and ran his hand across the big number seven on the back. He turned it over and had another look at the logo. It gave him a buzz to know that everyone agreed that 'the Wanderers' would be a good name for the team, so even though they wore blue, and even though he was playing on the other side of the world, he would still be playing for the Wanderers – the Pennendale Primary Wanderers.

The game was due to start at 4 pm, and by 3.50, Megs and the other Football Kids were changed and ready to go. Megs's stomach was beginning to tighten with nervous energy as he saw some of the other team warming up – soon it'd be all systems go.

School matches would usually be played earlier in the afternoon, but this one was organised especially so that everyone could come and support the team in their first game. Quite a few parents and friends were starting to mill about the sidelines in the sunshine, and now that school had finished Megs could see an army of Pennendale students being led by Mr Jackson towards the ground.

Paloma bounded over to give her dad a kiss. He'd already got the barbecue underway, and Vincent Braithwaite was standing beside him with drink in hand. Next to them were Paloma's and Megs's mums, chatting away as if they had known each other a lifetime. It was only Friday afternoon, but it was as if the weekend had already begun.

The pitch was in pristine condition, and Mr Morrison was busying himself putting up the nets just the way Megs liked them – reasonably firm, but with enough give in them so that when a goal was scored, the ball spun restlessly in the bottom of the net and didn't bounce back out. Megs didn't mind the boxed nets used in most big games, but hitting a loose net had a certain something about it, and his dad knew exactly what he meant.

It seemed everyone was helping out in their own way and, realising that, Megs began to feel a bit of pressure weighing on his shoulders. But he knew that if he wanted to become a professional footballer, it was a feeling he'd better get used to…

'Okay everybody, come quickly. Time for talk.' It was Atti, calling the team in for a meeting, and even though they'd been through the team plan at training in the week, it was time for the last minute instructions and reminders. Atti's relaxed style was in direct contrast to Mr Mac's professional approach back in England, but that didn't mean Megs was learning less than before. It was just that Atti didn't care if your boots were dirty and your shirt was untucked. 'Just play with heart, and feet will follow. Who cares what you look like?' was said more than once. But Val had shrewdly observed that Atti hadn't taken off his new team tracksuit top since he had been given it a few weeks earlier… and that it always seemed to be crisp and spotless.

They'd all been talking about it over the last week, but it was Max who had finally asked Atti why he limped. It was at their last training session before their first game, and Atti's answer was brief. Just that it came from an injury he'd picked up escaping from Hungary in 1956. He didn't say if that was why he hadn't played for so long, but they believed that one day he would tell them more. For now, though, everyone was just enjoying his enthusiasm and knowledge of the game.

The preparation for this match sure was different from the structured approach to the games Megs had played for the English Wanderers, but as he re-entered the change-rooms with his new friends, in his new blue uniform, to listen to his new coach, he had a special sense of a fresh beginning.

Perhaps an email he'd received from Mr Mac earlier in the week summed it up best:

Hi Megs,

It's been a while, but don't think that I've forgotten you! Word gets around – and your dad's been telling me what you've been up to. I'm glad you're going to get some competitive matches out there, but like I always told you back here, always do your best wherever and whenever there's a football. There's no better feeling than knowing you've given it all you've got.

So well done in getting the team together, and thanks for thinking of us... The Wanderers Down Under, huh!

All that's great, but once that whistle goes, it doesn't matter what colour you play in, who you are, how your team was formed or what country you're in. All that matters is that football – so go and get it!

All the best,

Mr Mac

The End...

Q and A with Mark Schwarzer

Some primary school kids from Essendon North in Victoria had the following questions for Mark, and we thought you would all like to see his answers. You can send yours to mark@megsmorrison.com.

Ruby

Q *Is being a superstar all it's cracked up to be?*

A In my mind I'm not a superstar. To my children I'm just Dad and to my friends and family I'm just a regular guy with an irregular job. But yes, life is great and I'm really lucky to make a living out of my hobby and passion.

Of course there is always a trade-off, so for every high along the road to 'superstardom' there have been a few lows. The highs are very high – like qualifying for the World Cup, and the lows are very low – like not being picked for the Croatia match. I've had to live away from home for a long time which is sometimes hard, and injury and defeat can be soul-destroying. But football has opened up so many opportunities and has given me options in life. I wouldn't swap it for anything in the world!

Srishti

Q *When did you start playing soccer, and where did you start?*

A Aged six at Colo Soccer Club in the western suburbs of Sydney.

Q *Is soccer your passion, your life, or your career?*

A It's my passion, my career and my hobby. But my life is my family.

Q *How do you celebrate a good win?*

A At club level there are so many games that after a good win it's normally 'head down' and start concentrating on the next match. At national team level, I normally have the opportunity to meet up with relatives back home whom I haven't seen for a while. We have a good catch-up and a drink.

Q *How do you deal with soccer bad times?*

A It's been a long road since I was 6! I've dealt with them by focusing on what's good in my life – especially my family. Mostly, I would say, rather than dwelling on my problems, I've tried to take action to fix them. For example, when I was third goalkeeper in Kaiserslautern and going nowhere fast, rather than dwell on my misery I chose to leave Germany for a fresh start in England. So action rather than passive contemplation is the way to move on.

Will and Kathleen

Q *When did you get asked to play for the Socceroos?*

A 1993 – World Cup Qualifier versus Canada, fourteen years ago!

Michael

Q *I am a goalie; how do you decide which way to jump?*

A You stand up as long as possible and try to judge where the shot will go.

Shaelyn

Q *Have you always wanted to be a soccer star? If not, what did you want to be before starting soccer?*

A I've never pursued stardom. I started out playing football as a young boy because it was something that I loved doing. When I met Pele at the Under-16s World Cup I realised that I wanted to make a career of it. But no, I never set out to be a star.

Tim

Q *How do you fall when you dive, so that you don't get hurt?*

A With proper coaching and correct technique you gradually learn to do it so as to minimise the risk of injury.

Matt

Q *Was the team you first played for really good?*

A No, we were just a regular, half-decent side.

Q Who was your best mate from that team?

A Greg Brown and Darren Mison at Colo Soccer Club.

Q Who is your best mate from the Socceroos?

A I don't have a best mate. They are all good team-mates.

Q Who was your favourite coach?

A Nick Sokaloff – my goal-keeping coach at Marconi.

Q When you are older what are you going to do?

A Coach an under-10s side in the eastern suburbs of Sydney and turn up to everything my kids are involved in – birthday parties, sports days, Sunday football matches and tennis matches, school plays etc. So far, having a career in football hasn't allowed me to make it to many of those things.

Maddy

Q How did you cope travelling around the world for the World Cup and losing?

A I don't consider what we achieved at the World Cup to be a 'loss'. We won in so many ways ... we won the hearts and minds of millions of Australians and raised the profile of football in Australia and abroad; we scored Australia's first ever World Cup goal and won our country's first ever World Cup match; and we were knocked out by the ultimate World Cup champions. So the travel paled in significance beside all those achievements.

David

Q Is it hard work to be a professional soccer player?

A Yes, to be good at anything consistently comes only from hard work. There has to be a lot of focus, commitment, perseverance and sacrifice to make it as a professional soccer player. But achieving your goals makes it all worthwhile.

Alex

Q How many days do you train a week?

A Five to six days a week, eleven months of the year, plus games.

Q *Can you eat what you want or can't you eat certain things?*

A I just always eat a healthy balanced diet. They say 'garbage in, garbage out', so I try to eat only good food.

Darcy

Q *How old are you?*

A Thirty-four.

Q *What do you prefer – being GK or being on the field?*

A GK – too much running involved in playing on the field.

Q *How did you feel when Australia was eliminated from the World Cup?*

A Devastated, but not for long. I tried to focus on the positive things we've achieved which soon made me cheer up.

Q *What position should I play? I'm a good goalie but also a good striker.*

A Follow your heart... whichever one gives you the biggest buzz.

Luis

Q *If you were not a soccer player what would you like to be?*

A There's nothing else I've ever wanted to be. I've committed so much of my life to football that I couldn't imagine being anything else.

Q *What would be the best moment in your life so far?*

A The birth of my children and World Cup qualification.

Andrew

Q *If you could be a fruit, what would you be and why?*

A Watermelon ... hard on the outside but soft on the inside.

About the Authors

Mark

It is nearly a decade now since Mark Schwarzer established himself as not only Australia's premium goalkeeper, but one of the world's best. With his quick reactions and innate composure, Mark has taken his career from humble beginnings in rural New South Wales to become a mainstay of what most sportspeople consider the greatest football league in the world, the English Premier League.

After spending his school days at North Richmond Primary and Colo High School, Mark made his impact on the Australian League (then the NSL) at the age of nineteen, and quickly entrenched himself as a regular by guiding his side, Marconi Fairfield, to the NSL championship. Mark's talent was quickly recognised by overseas scouts and at the age of twenty-one he was signed by Dynamo Dresden in Germany. After temporary stops at clubs Kaiserslautern and Bradford City, Mark found his home at Middlesbrough where the wiry Australian is now the longest-serving player and has notched over 300 matches.

Mark's heroics in the penalty shootout that got Australia to the 2006 World Cup will forever be remembered as a highlight in Australian sport, but they were just a small part of his ongoing Socceroo story that began with penalty saves against Canada in 1993.

Mark is just under two metres tall (6 foot 5 inches), has worn the same pair of shin pads since turning professional as a nineteen-year-old in 1992, and speaks three languages (English, German and Spanish). He lives in the north of England and is married to Paloma. They have two children, Julian and Amaya. After living in Europe since 1994, he looks forward to the day when the family will come home to Sydney's sunny shores.

Neil

Neil Montagnana Wallace was born in Australia, but his father is Scottish, his mother is English and his brother is American. His wife is Italian-Australian, and when they got married, they decided to stick their names together and make the most confusing surname in the world.

Neil was a handy soccer player who didn't make it in England, but still plays in Victoria's State Leagues. He's a Senior Licence coach, and wrote *Our Socceroos* in 2004 (www.oursocceroos.com) - which was how he struck up a friendship with Mark and ultimately how the seeds of Megs were sown. Earlier, he was Marketing and Events Manager at the Football Federation of Victoria.

The young Neil grew up in Castle Hill, NSW where he attended Castle Hill Primary and James Ruse before moving to Melbourne and going to Melbourne High School. After living in Rome in 2005, Neil now speaks Italian, and has learnt to enjoy olives. He lives in Melbourne with his wife Val and young son, Finn, a cat called Flash and a rabbit named Harry. When not writing, Neil is the Marketing and Strategy Director of Woof Creative Solutions.

In England Neil supports Coventry City; in Italy he supports Roma; in Scotland he supports Dunfermline and in Australia he supports Melbourne Victory. His record for juggling is 891, and his career highlight was one glorious training session years ago where he managed six beautiful nutmegs.

Join the Club

With so much interest in Megs, we've decided to form a *Club* to provide all sorts of extra information, exclusive and personal Mark Schwarzer video and diary entries, advanced extracts of future Megs books as well as 'behind the scenes' information from the authors.

Membership is *FREE*, so register now on www.megsmorrison.com.

Competitions, news, information and games are also all online for you to enjoy.

You can also contact us via email...

Neil Montagnana Wallace	neil@megsmorrison.com
Mark Schwarzer	mark@megsmorrison.com
Megs Morrison	megs@megsmorrison.com
Paloma	paloma@megsmorrison.com
Val	val@megsmorrison.com

You never know, maybe you'll see your name in print the next time around.

Mark, Neil, Megs and the Vootball Kids would all like to hear from you!

Shop Online
The Megs Shop not only sells copies of Megs and the Vootball Kids, it also has other books by the authors, a range of Megs merchandise, and a whole bunch of special offers.

www.megsmorrison.com

Coming Soon...

Scarves, Sombreros and Diving Headers

After a 5-0 demolition of Bayside Blues in Pennendale Primary's first real match, Megs was on cloud nine. Particularly after he bagged a hat-trick with half the school watching. But after scouring the papers for Val's report, he was disappointed to see that there was only a couple of lines in the Pennendale Press next to the lawn bowls results and above an ad for "Barb and Pete's Bloomin' Great Nursery". Not quite the big time Megs was expecting, it must be said.

But Megs's competitive spirit would soon be tested when his new Wanderers team discovers a major prize awaits the year's Champions. Especially when Pennendale's arch rivals hatch a mean-spirited strategy to ensure things are made as difficult as possible. Will the 'Vootball Kids' band together in the face of adversity? Will Megs remain focused on football whilst having to face some spiky issues at home? And what lessons will the game (and their new coach!) teach the 'Vootball Kids' this time around?

Book Two in the Megs series is about dealing with rascism, tackling adversity, and striving for shared goals. Oh yeah... and there's also new tricks, bags of fun, and plenty of pulsating football action along the way!

EDWARD *Megs* MORRISON

www.megsmorrison.com

Also by the Authors...

our**socceroos**

By Neil Montagnana Wallace
Published by Random House
www.oursocceroos.com

BUY ONLINE NOW at megsmorrison.com

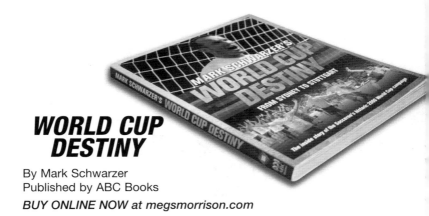

WORLD CUP DESTINY

By Mark Schwarzer
Published by ABC Books

BUY ONLINE NOW at megsmorrison.com